KNIGHTS

This book is a work of fiction. References to real people, events, establishments, organizations, or locales are intended only to provide the sense of authenticity and are use fictitiously. All other characters, all incidents, dialogue are drawn from the author's imagination and are not to be seen as real.

Copyright © 2018 by Dark Titan Entertainment. All rights reserved.

Published by Dark Titan Entertainment.

Dark Titan Universe is a branch of Dark Titan Entertainment.

First Printing 2018. Printed in the U.S.A.

ISBN: 978-0-999-82040-7

darktitanentertainment.com

KNIGHTS

TY'RON W. C. ROBINSON II

UNIVERSE

<u>DEATH IN RETROPOLIS</u>

Rain poured down on the city of Retropolis. The thunder roars through the clouds from the streaks of lightning. Vehicles move down the crowded city streets. Some held at red lights. Around the corner, two police cars speed down another street, chasing another vehicle, of what appears to be a dark violet Camaro. The police sharply turn corners to trap and inch closer to the Camaro.

"I can't tell who's driving the car. But I know it's a female." An officer says through the intercom.

"We're on her." An officer responded from the second car.

Chasing the Camaro through the streets and nearly hitting passengers and bystanders on sidewalks, they take a sharp left turn and immediately from another angle, a slick black and silver vehicle bolts out from the shadows. The vehicle speeds with great velocity toward the

1

Camaro as the officers look onward.

"What kind of car is that?" An officer said.

Inside the slick vehicle is The Swordman—Known only as an urban myth to the civilians, yet is written in the eons of history. Geared in his black and gray armor and cloaked hood.

His sword laying in the passenger seat. His face covered completely like a ninja with only his eyes visible, appearing completely white, reflecting off thee light source from the outside. He speeds up closer to the Camaro. The woman in the Camaro, takes notice of the slick car through the mirror. She sighs, rolling down the window, with a gun in hand. She looks back and starts shooting toward The Swordman.

The gunshots had no effect. The Swordman sat in his car calm. Somewhat somber. Still focused on the mission at hand. The woman, now aggravated, increases the gas attempting to drive out of The Swordman's sight. The Swordman, realizing the woman's plan, flips a switch near the steering wheel.

"Ejecting." The vehicle said.

The Swordman ejected from the vehicle, his black cloak flowing through the windy rainfall as he lands atop the Camaro. The woman starts to swerve the car around the streets, attempting to knock off The Swordman from the car. He holds tightly due to his mechanical and Kevlar-laced gloves attached to his dark golden gauntlets as his cloak continues flowing in the stormy winds. He removes a sharp object from his right gauntlet, which appears to be a silver dagger, yet, bulkier than an average dagger. He slams the dagger into the top of the car, slowly cutting it open.

"Damn it!" The woman screamed.

She placed her foot on the breaks, stopping the Camaro. The car stopped, and she jumped out, running away. The Swordman jumped from the car, staring at the woman. She continued running and The Swordman jumps in front of her. The woman pauses as he grabs her by her arms, places her in handcuffs. He walked her to the car and sat her next to the back of the Camaro. She sighs of disappointment. The Swordman looked at her, thinking in his mind to begin an interrogation. While reading her, the first thing he notices is her dark black hair with violet highlights and her pale skin.

"Who are you and what is your business here?" The Swordman asked.

"I am here for you of course." She said. "Why else would I come to a city like this. You're the main attraction around here and I attracted you."

"State your purpose, woman." The Swordman demanded.

"My purpose aligns with your purpose. We are one and soon you'll understand what that entails."

Police sirens came from the distance. They grew as the siren lights could been seen heading toward the location. The Swordman noticed the police and turned back toward the woman. She smiled at him as if she's seen someone special.

"Who are you?" The Swordman asked.

"I'm what has existed since the Fall of Man. That's who I am."

The sirens louder and increasingly closer. The Swordman knows he can't stay for much longer. His car appears from around the corner. He jumps in and drives off, disappearing from the location and leaving the woman sitting by the Camaro in handcuffs. The police arrive at the scene and they run toward her, guns pointed as they stand in front of her. They see the handcuffs. They know she is not a threat.

"Did another office leave her here or something?"

"No telling."

They raise her up, walking her to their police car. Another car arrived and two of the detectives exit the vehicle. Justine Copeland, one of the more focused women of the force and Cash Hankinson, a cocky, arrogant detective looking for the next big break in the field. Smoking a cigarette. He looks around the area for any trace of the slick black and silver vehicle that was reported during the chase, not finding any eminence what's so ever.

"Who do you think was driving that black and silver car?" Cash said.

"Someone with a lot of money in their possession." Justine said. "Who else could afford a car of that size and that detail."

They close the door on the woman in the back of the police car and leave the scene.

The police took the woman to Pegasus Prison, a place for the deadlier prisoners and the criminally insane. The officers decided to leave her in the prison until the appointed time for the proposed scheduled court date. Commissioner James Austin of the Retropolis Police Department entered Pegasus to speak with the female. Gaining access to her cell, one security officer walks Austin down the corridor toward her room. Stopping in front, he spoke with her through the cell door. Placing one hand in the pocket of his khaki trench coat and holding his hat in the other. He stared at her sitting in the corner of the room, smiling and giggling. He stood confused. Unsure of how to start a conversation.

"May I ask why are you giggling?"

"Because my time has fully begun."

"We didn't get your name. What is it?"

"My name? Why would you want to know my name? You should see it based on my appearance, Commissioner."

"From what we've gathered from the small witnesses downtown, you were apprehended by this "Swordman" figure. Is this true?"

"It is true."

"Did you tell this "Swordman" figure your name and your purpose here?"

"The Swordman." She said softly. "Him. I didn't tell him my name, but I did tell him my purpose aligns with his. Just like the stars on a special occasion."

Commissioner Austin looks at her, noticing her black hair and pale skin. He thinks for a moment. She only stares at him with her pale green eyes and a smile on her face from her black lipstick covered lips. Nothing comes to the Commissioner's mind but confusion and uncertainty.

"Still can't figure it out, Commissioner?" She said.

"I'm doing the best that I can right now. Thank you."

"It should be obvious as left to right." She said enthusiastically.

He shook his head, placing his hat on. He turns, walking down the corridor. She notices him leaving and runs toward the door. Her face close to the small bar space.

"Where are you going?!" She yelled. "Don't you want to know?!"

"I'll find out sooner or later." He replied. Not turning back toward her room.

The Commissioner leaves the cell floor as she begins to laugh. Disturbing everyone around her cell block and on the floor.

The Swordman sat within the Swordlair, an underground base built by his ancestors and enhanced by him for the modern age. Looking through the archives, searching historical details which may pertain to the woman. Not finding any trace of any kind, he decided to go into the archives of the Order of Swords, a creed of which he is the current leader and commander. His wife, Allison comes down the stairs into the lair. She saw him searching the archives. Glancing through the aged books.

"Kenari, why are you searching the archives?"

"Something is going on that involves the Order. Something strange and unusual in this generation."

"Are you speaking of that woman you stopped earlier tonight?" She said with notice.

"I am." He said with a nod. "She is not of this world. I felt it when I gazed into her eyes. There's something very ancient about her and its powerful. Life-threatening."

"So, tell me, what are your plans on finding out who or what she is?"

"The police have put her in Pegasus. I'm going there to have a word with her personally."

Allison sighed. Walking toward him, coming closer as she reached out to him, holding his arm.

"Are you sure it's a good idea? The police have already set a manhunt for you and others of the Order. What happens when they come across you?"

Kenari turned toward Allison. He smiled. Walking to the armory, he grabbed his sword, which hanged from the wall like a trophy. He held up his sword, known as

The Sword of the Elohim, placed it on his back into its sheath.

"If they use force, necessary precaution will be dealt."

Preparing to head out, Kenari kissed his wife and put on his cloaked hood and cowl, leaving the Swordlair in the slick car, named the Rapid-Blade, although the civilians of Retropolis who have seen the vehicle and know of its connection to The Swordman have jokingly refer to calling it the "Swordmobile". He drove to Pegasus Prison.

Upon arriving at Pegasus, sneaking himself into the prison and searching for the woman's cell. Going from floor to floor and hallway to hallway, he found her cell. Unlocking the door, he entered. Closing the door silently, he faces the woman who is still sitting in the corner of her cell.

"It is best that you tell me what you're doing here and what is going on."

"I knew you would come here to see me." She said with passion. "Can't resist huh."

"Who are you and why are you here? I can feel an ancient power upon you. Your spirit appears to be millennia old and its dark. Very dark."

"Amazing. No one can just look at me and figure out my name. I wear it on me every day."

The Swordman paused for a moment and meditated

on the thoughts and intent of the woman's mind and heart. He slowly started to comprehend who she is and why she is in Retropolis in this time. She glared up toward him, smiling. Reading him.

"You've figured it out haven't you. You are my kind of man."

"You've been here since the Fall of Man. You're not the Serpent of the Garden. You're not Lucifer himself. In so, that would make you Sin or Death."

She smiled, laughing with a slow clap.

"That's right, silly. You can call me Death."

"Death." The Swordman said., taking in his words.

"Sin leads people to me."

She laughed harder than previously before causing attention to come to her cell. The Swordman took a glance outside the door, seeing the security officers walking down the corridor. He turned to Death with serious intentions.

"You're the prophecy of our time. The one who will become the deadly enemy."

"No, I'm not. I'm no threat of your little creed."

"Then, what are you?"

"I'm *your* enemy."

"Is that so?"

"Yes, it is so. This is between you and me. Just as it was Lilith and Adam and Jezebel and Elijah. This is me and you. Until the earth's days are finished."

The Swordman nodded. Hearing the footsteps of the

security inching closer.

"Be that as it may. Just remember that I will stop you in all your devious works."

"I'm counting on it." Death said nodding and smiling. "Surely I am counting on it."

The Swordman left Death's cell as the officers approached. The officers look inside the cell, seeing only Death in the corner, laughing and giggling.

"What's with this woman?" One officer said.

"She's just another crazy nut."

Her laughter made the officers uncomfortable as they walked past her cell. Returning to their duties.

"Choose your Sins." Death said, rocking herself back and forth with a smile. "Choose your Sins."

<u>ALLIANCE SETTLED</u>

I

For over a year, Taltus—a titagod born from a place called Titanon amongst Mount Olympus has been praised and glorified by most of humanity for his selfless attitude of protecting the people of earth. The humans do not call him by his birth name, in turn they've coined him the name of The Powerman. Other names are the Man of Titans and the Titan of Tomorrow, declaring he's the savior the world needs in this hour. Taltus spends most of his time meditating afar from civilization. Occasionally, he will oversee Enigma City, the sister city of Retropolis.

Inside the Enigma City News Headquarters, Stephanie Vale, a young and beautiful reporter and mythologist delved into the mysteries of The Powerman and his origin which trace back to Greek Mythology. Her assistant, Alex Havens, a young man full of vigor walked into her office, handing her a book filled with firsthand accounts of civilians meeting The Powerman in dire situations.

"Are they real?" Stephanie said, flipping through the book.

"Yes ma'am." Alex said. "I wouldn't bring you false information to ruin your career."

"It's not ruining my career. It's only holding it down."

She opened the book and flipped the pages, scanning the documentations of The Powerman. Stopping on one page where the civilian named Anna West detailed a conversation between herself and The Powerman. The civilian stated The Powerman's parents are a titan and a goddess.

"A son of a titan and a goddess." Stephanie said. "Impressive."

"Guess that's where the term "*titagod*" came from."

"I'm sure, Alex." She said with a smile.

Stephanie read the address of the civilian. She shuts the book, putting it into her bag. She grabbed her things as she prepared to leave the office. Alex walking behind her, pacing her fast walking, following her to the elevator.

"Where are you going now, Ms. Vale?"

"I'm going to speak with this Curtis and Anna West family. They seem to know more about our Powerman than anyone else we know."

Stephanie entered the elevator. Alex turned around facing the office and the surrounding employees. He scratched his head before heading down the hallway toward the stairs.

One of the biggest corporations in the world named KexInc. is having a special meeting with its board of directors, and CEO and founder, Kenneth Kexlor Kendrick. Preferring to use the name, "Kex Kendrick". He sat at the table wearing his traditional white suit as his shoulder length blonde hair stood out amongst the other board members. Kex rubbed his chin, watching the board members preparing themselves. He scoffed.

"When can we start this meeting?" Kex said.

"In a moment, sir." One board member replied.

"We had it planned to begin approximately three minutes ago and yet none of you appear to have prepared yourselves. Why is that?"

"We wanted to make sure we had everything ready before coming into the meeting. To avoid confusion at all cost."

"I can understand your meaningful reasoning. But I do not accept it because of that fact. Can we start this meeting now? Because I have other business ventures to go and seek."

"Yes, we can."

The board started the meeting as Kex looked onward at the members and took a glance outside the window. After two and a half hours, Kex continued his stare outside the window. His personal assistant, Beatrice Mercer, a young woman stood at the boardroom entrance. She saw Kendrick at the window. Taking in a breath, closing the boardroom doors. She walked toward him.

"Is there something wrong, Mr. Kendrick?"

"No, Beatrice. There's nothing wrong. I just like to look and see the city from this angle. For what it really is and what it has become. Before that "titagod" appeared before us, this city was striving. It was successful and drew a crowd of many to itself. It presented opportunities for all who were seeking it."

"Isn't the city still that way now? Many come here for their own dreams and fulfillments."

"True, they still do. But, now they come for a very different reason. They come here to see that "Powerman" in the sky, hoping to become like him when they grow up. Grown men and women who behave like adults on their own turfs, suddenly come here and become like little children when they see him flying in the sky. Dreaming of becoming like him. Weakening themselves in the process and any offspring that they may bring about."

"The Powerman appears before them as a force of good. A physical force of good. One they can see."

Kex turned to Beatrice with a hint of laughter. The tension in his eyes could be felt by Beatrice herself. She knew deeply Kex was upset over The Powerman's appearance before the world of man. Believing it to have stolen his spot as the beacon of hope for mankind. It ate Kendrick up from the inside. Like a disease growing at a sluggish rate.

"Yet, what happens on the day when tragedy strikes him? What happens when he's not on his best day? What happens when he turns and sees us as the enemy? Those are the questions his followers need to ask themselves."

"You can spread these messages and warnings, Kex. You have that kind of power. The world knows of you and they will listen to you."

"They will hearken for a split second before The Powerman appears before them and they immediately become docile. Jesus, look at the world we live in now. From the armored man flying around the east coast, to a resurrected soldier in the Canadian military, to a cloaked swordsman running amok in Retropolis, to these rumors of a millennium god from another dimension, and now with this Powerman. Ugh! Humanity is falling, Beatrice. Following false gods has always been humanity's downfall."

"Then let them. Let them fall and when the time comes, they will be looking for someone to help them up again and you can be the man to do it. A true savior."

Kex glared at Beatrice. A glimmer of hope in his eyes

as he stared.

"You are correct, Beatrice." He said with a smile. "That's why I love to keep you around."

"You keep me around for a plethora of things, Kex."

"Indeed, I do."

She stepped closer to Kendrick. He grabbed her by the waist as she sat on his lap. She leaned in toward him, and they kissed. Kex stood up, laying Beatrice atop the table as they continued to kiss.

Stephanie drove out into the outskirts of Enigma City, entering the rural areas. Stopping at one house and looks at the address. She pulled out the sightings book, turning the pages. On the page from earlier, she saw the exact address. She walked toward the front door. She rang the doorbell, waiting patiently. The door opened and stood a man in his sixties.

"Yes ma'am. What can I do for you?" He said politely.

"I'm Stephanie Vale from the Enigma News and I'm here to see a Curtis and Anna West."

"Why would you want to see them?" He questioned.

Stephanie brought out the book. Showing him.

"Because they're in this book of civilians. Documenting their sightings of The Powerman. I'm here because I would really love to speak with them about it."

The man looked around the yard, scouting the location. He measured Stephanie with a stern face.

"You're the only one here?"

"Yes sir."

"Come in." He said with a nod.

Stephanie entered the home as the man closed the door. Inside the house, a woman in her late fifties was sitting down. Stephanie took another glance at the man and back toward the woman. She started to draw the conclusions.

"Wait a moment. Let me get this correct. You two are Curtis and Anna West? Correct me if I'm wrong about that."

"Ms. Vale, you are correct." Curtis said. "I had to be sure you were alone before allowing you into our home."

"Why does this woman want to speak with us, Curtis?" Anna said.

"It's about Him."

Anna sat quietly while Curtis stared at Stephanie. She doesn't know what to make of the whole situation as she just sat down in one of the seats and stayed calm.

"What do you want to know about him, Ms. Vale?" She asked.

"I want to know where he came from and what he is. I hear the term, "Titagod" being thrown around ever since he appeared. I read here that he's the son of a titan father and a goddess."

"Yes." Anna said. "Yes, he is."

"His real parents were named Hypernon and Sifera. They were residents in the city of Titanon that sits nearby Mount Olympus. A city of peace and harmony. Another Olympia you could call it. Until the Greek Gods discovered that titans, gods, and goddesses were intermingling with each other. Creating what we know of now as titagods and some goditans."

"What's the difference between a titagod and a goditan?" Stephanie said.

"A titagod is the product of a titan father and a goddess." Anna said. "A goditan is the product of a god and a titan mother."

"Zeus killed most of them and banished a few. The Powerman that you know of was one of the ones that was banished when he was only an infant. We do not know if his biological parents are still alive. But, there's a possibility that he knows."

"Do you know where I can find him?"

"I do. But I don't think he'll allow a human into his dwelling place."

"Why is that? He has helped humanity for over a year now. I would guess that it wouldn't be a problem if one were to come to him on their own."

"Take our advice, Ms. Vale. Let him come to you. Not you going to him. He has an order of how this thing works."

Stephanie grinned.

"Well, I'll like to thank you for taking the time to speak with me. It was a pleasure."

Stephanie stood up from the seat.

"Same here." Anna said. "Take care now."

"You too." She said smiling.

Stephanie exited the home, walking to her car. Getting into her vehicle, she thought for a brief minute before driving off their land, returning to the road.

Back at the KexInc. Headquarters building, in a room that is underground. Kex sat by himself in a chair facing a screen. The screen flickered on and off as a voice echoed through the screen. Fighting against static.

"Kex Kendrick." The statically voice said. "Have you received the object that he sent you?"

"I have." Kex said.

Kex reached underneath the desk, raising up a box. The box made of gold and wood. Kex reached and pulled a key from his coat pocket.

"When I do this, will our alliance be settled?" He asked, placing the key atop the box.

"It will, Kex Kendrick. The alliance between you, I and he will be settled into the stones of time. Open Pandora's Box and release the monster from within."

Kex placed the key into the box, unlocking it. A click is heard as Kex slowly opened it. A bright light shined from it, causing the room itself to shake as if an earthquake had took place. The vibrations of the box began to spread across the ground and tremble through the entire building. The tremble reached into Enigma

City and the surrounding areas. A screeching roar came from the box as a large figure bolted and flew through the ceiling, leaving nothing but a large hole. Kex stared.

"What was that?" Kex said trembling. "I didn't see what it was. But, it was large."

"Don't worry about that. It will solve this Powerman problem of yours and ours."

"That's all I need to know."

Out in an area not known to many humans, stood a large fortress. Covered in ice with walls made up of a material not known to man, yet glowing a mid-blue aura. The fortress is called the Fortress of Cytron and is the dwelling place of The Powerman. Inside the fortress are placed a variety of titanonian weapons and gear, relics from the Greek Gods. In the main area of the fortress sat Taltus. Sitting in a throne room of sorts. Quiet and silent. The trembling from Pandora's Box had reached the fortress. Taltus' eyes opened after the tremor ceased, glowing a golden yellow resembling lightning. He stood from the chair and flew from the fortress, surpassing jet speed.

II

Enigma City began to quake as the tremor from Pandora's Box grew stronger. Civilians ran amok in the streets searching for shelter. A screech is heard from the sky and the civilians saw a large figure. The figure appeared to have a physical mixture of a dragon and a gargoyle. The beast flew toward the civilians, clawing at them and attempting to snatch them from the ground. The creature flew through the city, frightening the people.

From the Enigma News building, Stephanie saw the creature and recognized it from her mythological studies. Alex also saw the creature, immediately taking photos of the monster.

"What is that thing?" Alex asked.

"The Greeks called it Drago." Stephanie said. "It's a hybrid beast between a gargoyle and a dragon. Known by ancient scholars as the mutant gargoyle. Zeus created the monster and endowed it with his own power and later placed the creature into Pandora's Box. We've come to know it as the Dragon Gargoyle."

The Dragon Gargoyle wiped its claws toward the civilians as it flew low in the air only a few feet away from the ground. In the distance, Kex and Beatrice watched the event take place from the boardroom office.

"Is this what you wanted Kex?"

"This is the beginning of what I want." Kex said with

his hands together. Savoring the moment.

The Dragon Gargoyle fought off the Enigma City Police Department as they came out and started firing at the creature. The bullets ricochet toward them and their cars. Bouncing off the creature dense and scaly skin. The police are aware that their weapons can do no harm to the creature. The creature roared into the air. After which a sonic boom cracked from the clouds, gathering everyone's attention. The Dragon Gargoyle looked up and saw The Powerman flying down in great speed. Only his dark blue cape could be seen when flying at great speed by the civilians.

"There he is!" A civilian screamed.

The Powerman speared Dragon Gargoyle through the city streets and delivered a strong right punch to the creature, knocking him through the buildings. Seeing through the debris, Powerman grabbed Drago and pummeled it into the ground before throwing the creature into the air and flying toward it. Powerman went for another punch, and Drago saw it and swiped Powerman in the face and slammed him into the ground. Drago charged its hands up and started to throw thunderbolts toward Powerman. He dodged and swiped them out of his way before flying back toward Drago. Using its reflexes as much as it can, Drago punched Powerman and clawed at his white and blue armored suit before screeching in his face. Powerman snatched Drago by its throat, punching him in the abdomen and tossed him up into the air, hovered above him, releasing a double-handed slam toward the ground. Drago fell into the ground, leaving a small crater in the city road. Powerman slowly came down from the sky and stood on the road, staring at Drago.

"This is over." He said.

"This. This is far from the end!" Drago said.

The Powerman's eyes glowed gold as he projected from his eyes, lightning vision toward Drago, burning and electrocuting him until he was knocked unconscious. The civilians cheered for The Powerman's victory with Stephanie and Alex approached him. Powerman picked up Drago and before he flew off, he saw Stephanie and Alex and he could sense their internal fear.

"You don't have to fear me." The Powerman declared.

"You're incredible." Alex said in awe. "Just awesome."

Stephanie took a step closer. The Powerman held out his hand toward her. She stopped.

"If you're wanting to have a word with me. Please, do it another time."

"Sure thing." Stephanie said.

The Powerman showed a faint smile before flying into the air and out of the sight of the civilians. Stephanie and Alex looked in the sky, seeing how quickly he vanished from their presence. Alex is full of exciting emotions.

"That was the Man of Titans!"

"Our Chosen Son." Stephanie said. Acknowledging the feats of Taltus The Powerman.

Kex destroyed his office after seeing the Dragon Gargoyle's defeat by The Powerman. Beatrice only watched as he decimated much of his property. In the middle of the office, a beam of light appeared, frightening Beatrice as she held up an energy gun from her side. Kex stared toward the beam, inside the beam was Zeus, the Greek god of thunder himself. Long white hair and beard. Dressed in ancient Greek apparel and standing at a great height. Towering over Kex and Beatrice. Staring into the eyes of Kex. Beatrice is silence.

"Kex Kendrick. It's time you and I speak."

THE SCAVENGER'S HUNT

Inside of his Nano-bunker, Nathan Hawke—the CEO of Hawke Industries and known in the urban myths across the world secretly as The Nano Man. After being hit with a military weapon and put into a coma for three months, he was injected with bio-nanotechnology that repaired his body and enhanced his mental control. Giving him complete control over his nano-exoskeleton armored suit. Nathan has been The Nano Man for over two years now after stopping an old friend from destroying the city of Newark, New Jersey.

Hawke, now sitting in his bunker, doing more of his research into building his armored exposits, the process of becoming more efficient as time goes on. Increasing their strengths, speed, and agilities. Aside from his bulky armor, he develops a sleeker design, one that is lightweight compared to the first ones. Staring at the holographic designs of the suits, he thought to himself, deciding which of them should be next to build and the one to come afterwards.

"If I were to take this one and put in the same technology used during space missions, this suit could give the wearer the ability to breathe in space for nearly an unlimited amount of time. With some equations to solve of course."

Footsteps echoed in the entrance to the bunker. He turned around and saw his assistant Alice Jacobs approaching him from the entrance. She gazed around the bunker, spotting the six exo-suits completed by Hawke within a matter of three weeks and noticed the holograms, detailing the plans for the next pairs of suits.

She looked appalled at the speed of the suit's development. Hawke stared at her and showed off a smile.

"Don't you ever take a day off?"

"Is today vacation day?"

"I don't think it is."

"Then why take a day off, Alice."

"You're still building these suits and you know it will be only a matter of time before someone discovers this place and attempts to take them from you."

"That's not possible."

"How is that not possible when you're sporting around in these suits across the country?"

"Because I am The Nano Man. Simple. To take away the exo-suits, they'll have to take me as well. Because as you know, inside my body or my blood I should say, is the true source of the suits' power."

"You do understand that someone can and will replicate the bio-nano fibers that are in your body, right."

"Only someone with the intelligence that is equivalent to mine."

Derek Willis, Hawke's oldest assistant entered the bunker, walking toward Hawke and Alice. Wearing his standard casual suit with a red tie.

"Mr. Hawke, Mr. Jon Cramer insists you attend the board meeting today concerning the trade-off between your company and KexInc."

"Sure thing. Contact Cramer for me. Tell him that I will be there as soon as possible."

"Yes sir."

Willis left the bunker, Hawke stood up and walked to a nearby closet, opening it up, revealing a line of business suits. He scouted through them. Variety of colors. He turned over to Alice as if he's a young child picking out a toy.

"Which one do you think I should wear?"

"Why would that be up to me?"

"Because you know more about fashion than I do. Unless its tech-fashion."

Alice exhaled as she approached the closet, going through the suits. Hawke looked on and took a quick glance at his watch. Alice spotted him glancing.

"Is that a gesture for me to hurry up?"

"In a way. Yes."

She grabbed a suit from the closet and handed it over to Hawke.

"You're holding me up, Alice."

"I will see you at the car."

"Sure." Hawke said as he started to put on his suit.

In the car, Alice sat waiting for Hawke, the driver, Brian Neutron awaited Hawke from the entrance doors. He turned back to Alice, looking at her watch.

"What is taking him so long?" Brian asked, "Himself."

From the entrance of the Hawke Mansion came Hawke, wearing the suit, walking toward the car. He entered the car, sitting next to Alice in the back. Nodded to Neutron.

"I'm ready."

"Yes sir. Corporate office?"

"Exactly."

Neutron placed the car in gear and drove off the Hawke Mansion property. Inside the car, Alice handed Hawke a set of papers showing him the trade-off deal between his company and KexInc. He read the papers and turned to Alice.

"So, we've been doing all of this and we're just getting

the information back?"

"It's the second quarter results, Nathan."

"Oh. We're in the third quarter, correct?"

"Yes."

"No need to get upset. I'm just trying to find a better way at understanding these things."

"Have it programmed into your nano-suits. I'm sure you can keep track of them that way."

"Great idea."

They reached to the corporate office of Hawke Industries in downtown Newark, New Jersey. Taking the elevator to the top floor where the meeting is being held. Inside the elevator, Hawke held in his hand, a small device like a cell phone, yet, it's a device that is able to remotely control the Nano Man armor at will when in use. Alice saw it and snatched it from Hawke.

"What was that for?

"I don't think you'll need the suit for a business meeting."

"Well, you never know. What if one of them gets upset. You know, starts throwing stuff around. Armor yourself up."

Alice put the device in her purse. Hawke shook his head. The elevator opened as Hawke and Alice entered the meeting room. Seeing the board of directors from Hawke Industries sitting facing the board of directors from KexInc. Hawke searched around the room for the CEO of KexInc. and didn't see him.

"Where's the boss?"

"Mr. Kendrick is sorry to inform you that he couldn't make it to this event because of some business matters in Canada."

"Oh. So, Canada's business is more important than our business. Understandable."

Hawke sat at the table with the board members and Niles Valcrow, one of Hawke's business partners entered the room. Walking toward the table, he sat near Hawke.

"I am truly sorry that I am late, and I am even more sorry that Mr. Hawke beat me here."

"Sometimes you win and lose, Niles."

"Indeed, you do."

Hawke noticed Niles' new haircut as it was once much hair on his head, now its cut short near the scalp. His eyebrows now arched.

"I like the new hairstyle and look you have, Niles. It fits your personality."

"Likewise, I would say. Now let's get to business shall we."

While the business meeting taking place, in downtown Newark, an older man wearing an armored suit of his own, equipped with mechanical wings flew through the city, harming civilians and firing small missiles from his wrists at cars, exploding them. After several minutes, the police arrived at the scene and drew their guns at the man. The flying man stopped and hovered in mid-air over the officers.

"Come down and keep your hands up!"

The man lowered himself toward the street. Holding his hands up. The mechanical wings spread open as he swooped past the officers, knocking them down and against the cars as he returned into the air. The man flew throughout the downtown area, destroying anything he saw fit.

"This is a scavenger hunt and I am the scavenger." The man said. "Fear me and you will not be collected and feasted upon."

Civilians screamed and hollered in the city. Ducking and running from the flying mechanical winged-man.

Back at the office, Hawke's device started to beep in the middle of the meeting. Gathering everyone's attention as he slowly turned toward Alice, who stared at him.

"What?"

"It's beeping."

Alice went deep into her purse, seeing Hawke's device beeping with a flashing green light. She glared at Hawke and he grinned. Handing him the device. He looked. Opening a holographic news report. Seeing the news of the flying man downtown.

"Sorry, I have to go. it's a business call. Non-related to this meeting here."

"So, who's going to speak for you?" Niles asked. "We need to know so we can get the information back to you."

Hawke pointed toward Alice like a small child.

'Give Alice the details and she'll deliver them to me back at the mansion. No problems. No confusion."

Hawke left the room in the elevator. Inside the elevator, Hawke pressed a holographic button from the device and back at the bunker, the Nano Man armor awoke. The armor stood upright from its current base. Decked in layers of midnight teal and silver coloring. The driveway in the bunker opened, allowing the armor to fly out through an exit which resembled a small runway.

Hawke stood outside of the office, seeing the suit coming in the distance. He moved toward a secluded area by the office as the suit followed him, tracking the device's whereabouts. The suit landed in front of him. Hawke entered, and the suit consumed him. His voice changed. His witty behavior gone. Nathan is now The Nano Man. He flew up into the air, heading straight for downtown Newark.

In the suit's system is an A.I. commonly called NOVELL.

"Good to speak to you, sir." NOVELL said.

"NOVELL, feed me the info on this flying man downtown." Hawke said.

"Will do, sir."

The flying man continued his chaos downtown. The thrusts of the Nano Man behind him can be heard from a distance. He turned, looking, staring at him. Nano Man moved closer and stopped at a halt, facing the flying man. Nano Man examined the man's suit mechanics and design. Glancing at the wings extending from his back.

"You have a thing for birds?"

"I am here to scavenge on the food that it is my presence. The food that will be the dead corpses of Newark's people."

"You're a vulture?"

"I am not."

The flying man tackled Nano Man into a building, trying to rip his suit apart. Nano Man grabbed the man by his throat, slamming him into the ground and dragging him for a second before tossing him into a pair of cars sitting next to a sidewalk.

"Your suit is pretty impressive. Tell me, who gave you that suit?"

"A wealthy man with great intensions."

The man flew toward Nano Man and speared him into a building, holding onto him, flying higher up in the air. Nano Man noticed the city becoming smaller as they inch higher in the sky. The man laughed with a cough as he increased the height to the point of seeing the entire city of Newark from the sky. Nano Man uppercut him. Moving over, grabbing one of the wings. He held it tight and the wing started to tear. The suit's strength ripped off the wing.

"A bird can't fly without both wings."

The man fell from the sky. He inched closer to the ground, Nano Man captured him, placing him on the street and ripping out his suit's power source, leaving the man virtually powerless. Nano Man checked on the civilians nearby and the police came upon the scene before he flew off.

Back at the Nano-bunker, Hawke tells Alice about the flying man, whose real name is Oswald Peters. The city is now calling him—the *Geier*, due to finding information regarding the man's occupation with birds. Hawke discussed the power suit Geier wore and where he could've received the suit from. Not finding any close sources, he left the case unclassified for the moment.

Oswald sat inside a prison cell, hearing how the city is now calling him the Geier. He relished his new name, one he hoped will bring a great fear into the people. A visitor came to the cell. The cell door opened, the visitor entered, sitting down in front of Oswald with a serious look, expressing his anger and his curiosity at the same time. Oswald doesn't know what to make of this visit.

"Does he know?"

"He does not know." Oswald replied. "Mr. Hawke has no clue in any of this."

"Good. Let's keep it that way until the scheduled time." Niles said with a grin.

ADDER'S GAME

Running through the snow-filled Canadian forest, Adam Watson—codenamed Commander Norland lead his team of soldiers through the forest, in search of a hidden base that belongs to a terrorist organization only referred to as ADDER. Norland moves through the snow, running at rapid speed past the trees. One of the following soldiers, Woody Fields, also known throughout Canada with his codename, Canadian Hawk speaks to Norland.

"So, what is the game plan, Commander?"

"We find their base. We clean it out until there's not a single ADDER agent standing."

"Just like we did with Crimson Suk?"

"Just like that."

Woody nodded.

"I fully understand."

Speaking to Norland and his soldiers through their

radio communicators is General Sarge Hunter, one of the commanding generals in the United States. He is working alongside Norland with Canadian intelligence due to the amount of attacks ADDER has committed in the United States alongside Canada.

"Commander Norland. I need you to listen to me for a brief second before you find that base."

"What's the problem, sir?" Norland asked. "A decoy?"

"No decoy. Anton Kozlov is present at the base. Our eyes in the sky caught a glimpse of him entering the base with an army of his own. Best you take care of yourself and the others. No telling what Kozlov could be up to with making an alliance with ADDER."

"I understand you, General."

Steve Nixon, one of the other soldiers alongside Norland approaches him as they see the base buried within the trees before them. They take a moment to stop and rest before entering the sight. Steve looks around the forest.

"So, once we're in there, we take out every one of them. Permanently?" Steve said.

"Every last one. Do not leave a single person standing unless its Kozlov or Madame Cobra. Leave them alive so we can bring them to T.I.T.A.N. for interrogation."

"We understand you, Commander." Woody said.

They nod at one another before making their steps toward the ADDER base. Stepping onto the base's grounds, they notice the ground is covered in landmines, to avoid trespassers from coming closer to the base. Norland signals his team to circle around them in order to avoid a possible explosion, which would bring an army of ADDER soldiers to them.

"They laced this ground up didn't they." Woody said.

"Can't blame them, Fields." Steve said. "T.I.T.A.N. does the same thing at their hidden bases."

Taking a look towards the windows of the base, Norland can see Kozlov inside, dressed in his silver and white business suit, speaking with some of the ADDER soldiers, dressed in their dark green militaristic uniforms, possibly giving them instructions. Steve takes a look for himself, sees Kozlov and immediately he holds his rifle, preparing to take a shot. Norland notices Steve's motives and grabs the rifle. Pressing it down near the ground. Steve, wanting to gun down Kozlov is staring in the eyes of Norland.

"I understand you want to take him out. But you can't."

"He's a madman just like the rest of them. He has to go. We can kill him and bring Madame Cobra in for interrogation. Get rid of one and leave the last one for us."

"No. We bring them both back to T.I.T.A.N. understand. We do not leave one dead and the other alive."

Steve, trying slowly to calm himself down, holds his rifle down to his side. He gives Norland a slight, but unsure nod. Norland nods back with respect as he looks at the team.

"Are you ready?" Norland said to the team.

"Yes sir!" The team responded.

"Let's do this."

Norland and the team ran toward the base's entrance doors. Norland reaches the door and bursts them open, kicking them in. Upon the doors opening, they see nothing but ADDER soldiers standing before them.

"We have intruders!" One ADDER soldier yelled.

They all draw their firearms toward Norland and his team, facing them at the doors. Norland stares, counting the soldiers in his sight. before he raises his arm up. Giving his team the signal.

"Fire!" Norland yelled.

The team begin firing at the ADDER soldiers, engaging into hand-to-hand combat with some of them. The combating between Norland's team and the ADDER soldiers gets the attention of both Kozlov and Madame Cobra as they watch the brawl from a distance. Kozlov looks at the brawl and sees Norland, spotting his white and red military suit.

"It seems they've brought the Commander to ruin our little business engagement." Kozlov said. "We have to send in more soldiers."

"If the soldiers can't handle him and his fellows, leave them to me." Madame Cobra said. "I can take them alone if I have to."

Madame Cobra moved away from the window, leaving the room, proceeding to move closer to the brawl. Kozlov stands and watches the battle from afar. He gazes at Madame before turning his eyes toward Norland, who is single-handedly taking out most of the ADDER soldiers.

"I always have to deal with these kinds of people." Kozlov said. "Nevermore I say."

Kozlov walks over toward a desk and picks up a suitcase from underneath. He opens the suitcase, revealing a silver chromed skull mask. One of his treasured possessions. He picks up the mask, putting it on. He closes the suitcase and leaves the office area, walking towards Norland and his team. Madame Cobra and Kozlov slowly begin to approach them together, Norland and his team have defeated the ADDER soldiers and they're the only ones standing.

"Looks like we've done our job here." Steve said. "What's next, Commander?"

"We find Madame Cobra and Kozlov. Take them with us back to headquarters."

"Well, well. You people have done a fine job" Madame Cobra said as she stood in front of Norland and the team.

"Looks like she came to us, Commander." Woody said. "I call that an even playing field for us."

Norland locked his sights at Madame Cobra. Seeing her wearing a dark brownish-green uniform that is made of titanium-laced fibers. Its appearance is somewhat of a dress. Norland gazes around the open area of the base before locking his eyes on Madame Cobra's own green eyes. They pierce Norland's. He can feel how poisonous she truly is.

"Where's Kozlov?"

"I am right here, Commander Norland." Kozlov said as he entered the area from behind Norland. "In the flesh."

Norland saw the silver chromed skull mask Kozlov wore. The team unable to figure out its purpose, yet it presents a terrifying chill down their spines. Norland stands his ground, putting his handgun back into the holster and his other weapons in their place. He stands completely open, facing ADDER and Kozlov.

"You two have a choice to make. Either you both can come with us back to T.I.T.A.N. for interrogation or me and my team can beat you until you surrender."

"Interesting." Madame Cobra said. "How would an handsome fellow like yourself make me surrender to your will?"

"There's no time to flirt with the man, Madame." Kozlov said. "Let's kill them and go about our regular business schedule."

Madame turned her attention to Kozlov. Smiling as she turns back to Norland.

"I like his plan even more."

She raised up a machine gun from her uniform coat

and starts firing at Norland and the team. They run and duck behind the crates for cover as ADDER shoots at them. The machine gun blazing around them. Bullets flying over their heads. Kozlov watches and reaches into his coat pocket, pulling out a pistol of his own and starts firing at the crates himself.

"They'll be dead within a few minutes." Kozlov said.

"Let's be sure about that before we jump to conclusions, Anton." Madame said. "We should have fun with this."

"You can have your fun with them all you desire. I want to see them dead."

Behind the crates, Norland looks to Woody and his shield.

"Think you can get closer to them with your shield?" Norland said.

"I believe I can."

"Then do it and move fast."

Woody nodded, placing his shield in front of him, running toward Madame and Kozlov. They turned their firing toward him, trying to shoot through the shield.

"The fool is running right at us!" Kozlov yelled. "Get that shield out of the way!"

Woody moved faster toward Madame and Kozlov. Feeling the firepower increasing against his shield. Steve runs behind Woody and takes a shot at Kozlov's left leg with his handgun. The bullet goes through his leg. Kozlov jumps in shock from the wound, losing his balance and falling to the ground, holding his leg tightly. Madame Cobra stops firing as Woody shoves her with his shield to the ground.

"Damn it!" Kozlov screamed.

Norland approached them, knelling down toward Kozlov. Removing his skull mask to reveal his face. Kozlov stared at Norland with anger in his eyes. The rage within him could be felt inside the room. Woody and Steve apprehend Madame Cobra, placing her in handcuffs.

"You think taking me to T.I.T.A.N. will be the end of me, Commander Norland?!" Kozlov said. "Our journey has only just begun, boy!"

"I'm sure it has begun, Kozlov." Norland said. "I am highly sure of it."

Norland picked up Kozlov and handcuffs him. They exit the base and approach a pair of T.I.T.A.N. jeeps, driven by two T.I.T.A.N. agents. They put ADDER and Kozlov in the separate jeeps.

"Make sure they go directly to headquarters." Norland said to the agents.

"We will do that, Commander." The agent said.

The agents drive off of the premises as Norland and his team return to the T.I.T.A.N. headquarters in a jet called the hoverjet.

Several days after the base incident, Norland walks into one of the laboratories within the T.I.T.A.N.

headquarters base. Inside the laboratory is Professor John Flm. The wise doctor, wearing his white coat is greeted by Norland.

"Commander Norland. Good to see you here."

"Please, just call me Adam."

"Adam, it is." Flm said. "What brings you to my laboratory?"

"I've been having those feelings again. The urges from before. I do not know how to deal with them."

Flm sits Norland down at the table and sits in a chair facing him.

"From what we know, the lightning bolt that struck you in the battlefield during the Republic War should've killed you. But, you managed to survive it and through it, you've achieved great strength and abilities from it. I would in simple terms call it grace."

"How can I be sure it's grace and not a curse. There's no telling what these abilities can do when they're at their full strength."

"You said after you were struck, you were confronted by a man who was surrounded by ice and snow. A very, very cold place. You said he told you that you would have these abilities and would use them as a force for good. What is the problem with that?"

"I am only human. If I slip, these abilities that could be used as a force for good could eventually turn into a source for evil. I know I'm a flawed man. Just like everyone else."

"Not everyone else has the abilities you possess. Take some time and learn how to use them. They'll most likely suit you better on the field rather than using these modern-day weapons."

Norland took in Flm's words. Responding with a nod and a grin.

"Thanks for the information, Professor."

"Anytime, Adam."

Norland left the laboratory. Flm continues going back to his work on the desk. His work is in fact studying the silver chromed skull mask of Kozlov, who is being called throughout the headquarters as the Iron Crane. Flm takes a closer look at the mask through microscopic lenses. He saw the features within the texture of the mask. Resembling interstellar minerals such as meteor fragment and space dust. It intrigued Flm completely.

"I wonder how this mask was formed."

NOLDAR'S TRICKERY

I

Eragard, the first of the fifteen-dimensional realms to the Millennium Gods, ruled over by their all-father, Eden. Theus, the Millennium God of Thunder and the Son of Eden is the Prince of Eragard and the military commander, leading the Eragardian armies into battle while preparing himself to one day become the King of Eragard when the appointed time comes.

Theus, leading Lady Soya, the Millennium Goddess of War and the Mighty Trio, combined of Aslan, the Millennium God of Nature, Ornod, the Millennium God of the Brave and Bold, and Vanor, the Millennium God of Warfare and Violence made their way toward one of Eragard's open fields, primarily used for warfare. They approach, already having the knowledge of a battle, currently taking place between the Light Elves and the Dark Elves. Both sides have been warned about having their war on the fields of Eragard countless times in their history. Theus, approaching the commanding generals of both armies to get their situation straight. Theus, looked onward, seeing the elves in battle. Clashing each other with clubs and war hammers. Theus flies over toward them.

The elves continued their battle and gaze upward, seeing Theus hovering above them as his silver helmet shines and his dark blue cape flows with the wind. Erianor, the general of the Dark Elves pushed the elves aside to get in the center near Theus.

"Theus, Son of Eden!" Erianor yelled. "Why have you come and have chosen to interfere in our war against the Light Elves?"

"Take your warfare onto another realm's land, dark elf." Theus said. "This is Eragardian soil you're spilling elvish blood upon. We do not take it lightly."

Erianor waved his hand in a negative gesture toward Theus, mocking him and his words.

"Go back to your castle, Prince of Eragard and leave this battle to us to finish."

Erianor walked away as Theus stared at him. Theus' eyes slowly glow a thunderous blue with small fragments of lightning sparked from them.

"You did not heed my words, dark elf. I said leave!" Theus declared as he charged up a thunderbolt in his hand. Throwing it at Erianor, hitting him in his back. The bolt knocked Erianor forwards, falling to the ground after flying through the air by the strength of Theus' thunderbolt.

"You dare to assault me! A dark elf! How dare you, Son of Eragard!" Erianor said with anger. "You have made a big mistake for yourself, boy!"

Erianor and the remaining dark elves vanished into thick black smoke. Leaving only the light elves and their general, Eriador. Theus came down and approached Eriador.

"Seems you have more of a brain than your twin brother."

"Appears to be the case, Son of Eden. I will take my remaining brethren and we will leave your field at once."

"I thank you for your honesty and respect, General of the Light Elves."

Eriador created a portal made of elvish crystals. He and the light elves entered, returning to their realm in a flash of light. Leaving the realm of Eragard. The portal closed and Theus turned away, seeing Lady Soya walking toward him.

"What is it now, my Lady Soya?"

"You know the dark elves will return and Emperor Voldor might come alongside them this time."

"Then let him and his army come. We will deal with them ourselves. Maybe that's what the dark elves need. Some Millennium Gods to settle their score once and for all."

Theus flies into the air, returning to the city of Eragard and its palace.

In the wilderness outskirts of Eragard stood an abandoned castle. Aged and broken down. Within the castle sat Noldar, the Millennium God of Guile with his enchantress, Illianna, known as the Millennium Goddess of Sorcery. Noldar had remained quietly in the middle of the trodden down castle that once belonged to an ancient sorcerer. When Illianna walked by his side, gazing her eyes into the portal Noldar had been staring into. Moving her dark and wavy hair to the side behind her shoulder.

"What are you gazing at now, Noldar?"

"I am preparing to open the portal to release my army upon Eragard. Theus and his lackeys have already dealt with the elf war. Now they'll have to contend with the wrath of Jontheim's finest arsenal. Frost Giants."

"Will Aurgelmir be attending this little get together party?"

"Aurgelmir is the one who gave me the opportunity to control his army and lead them into Eragard. So that they may destroy all who live therein and take some spoils back to their realm with them."

"When are they coming through the portal?"

"Right after the moonlight hits the top of Eden's

golden palace."

In the portal Noldar and Illianna are staring into, they saw the army of frost giants, wielding frozen axes, hammers, and swords. Prepared and ready for Noldar's portal to open.

During the sundown in Eragard, Theus, Lady Soya, and the Mighty Trio entered the throne room where Eden and his wife, Meredith, the Mother of Theus and Queen of Eragard are sitting. They welcomed them into the throne room. They bowed before the king and queen of Eragard. Both wore their traditional royal garbs, paying honor and respect to the ancient Eragardians of old.

"Theus, our son." Eden said. "What is the news of the elves? Have they taken heed to the warning and left our borders as commanded?"

"The light elves did according to what we asked. But, the dark elves put up a fight. In truth, it was their general, Erianor. I took the small matter into my own hand and knocked him on the ground. Needed to make a statement. He didn't take kindly to it and said that he would return again to do battle with us or the light elves."

"Erianor has always been the stubborn, hotheaded creature of magic. Unlike his brother, Eriador, who has always shown respect toward us and any entities in the fifteen realms. Make sure that the dark elves to not return. Even if their emperor comes along with them."

Eden suddenly stares into space. For a moment, they question what he is seeing and after a while, Eden gets his focus back onto Theus and the others.

"Father, what is it?"

"Frost Giants are on their way! Make ready for war!"

Eden slammed his spear into the ground, trembling the castle and the surrounding areas of Eragard, awakening the people and the Eragardian soldiers. They made ready and stood outside of the palace, waiting for Eden to appear. Theus walked alongside his father as did Soya and the Trio.

"Frost Giants? How could they come here without anyone's notice?"

"Vindhler seen them coming through a portal. A portal made of dark magic and he sensed it toward me and gave me the warning. When you become King of Eragard, you will also have this power. As you have little of it now. You just don't know how to use it yet."

They moved outside the palace and could see the dozens of Eragardian soldiers, standing and prepared for battle. Eden turned to Theus, directing him to the soldiers.

"Take these soldiers and lead them into the battle with the frost giants. I know for certain that with you leading the way, they will be unstoppable."

"I will father."

Theus raised up his war hammer, known as the mystical hammer called Mithrandir. He held it up above his head.

"For the Realm of Eragard!"

The soldiers yelled the battle cry with Theus before heading off toward the portal in the distance fields of Eragard. Eden and Meredith watched Theus and the army march from the palace walls, entering the open fields.

"They've got this under control, Meredith. No need to concern yourself of this matter."

Theus and the Eragardian soldiers entered the open fields. Finding nothing in sight, Soya walked over to Theus as the Trio look around the fields.

"Where are the frost giants?"

"They're on their way. Just have to keep our eyes open."

"Who would allow them into our realm?" Soya asked.

"Our enemies. One crosses my mind."

A low thump echoed through the air as one of the soldiers screamed after being attacked and slammed by a frost giant's battle club. The portal revealed itself, with the frost giants stomping out in mass. All yelling and holding up their frozen weapons of war. Theus turned toward them as does the soldiers.

"Let's clean this field."

He flew toward the frost giants, diving right through them with the hammer in front. Going straight through the frost giants, cutting off limbs and ramming through the abdomens of a few. Lady Soya fought the frost giants with her sword called the Stormslasher. The trio battled the front giants in their fashionable pairs of three. Aslan killed them with his battle sword, Ornod used his battle club, knocking off their heads as he encountered, and Vanor with his battle sword, slaughtering the frost giants, leaving only their limbs remaining on the ground, melting away without a hint of heat.

Theus hovered in the sky and stretched out his arms, conjuring a miniature thunderstorm above the battlefield. Only a little moonlight was able to shine upon the battlefield. The lightning intensified as Theus directed the lightning against the frost giants. Lightning struck down upon the frost giants, who roared in pain. Their bodies in an intense burning sensation.

"Now, you will understand why I am called the Millennium God of Thunder!" Theus declared. "Now, feel the power of the storm!"

Heavy rain poured down from the clouds as the lightning struck many of the frost giants. Most made the attempt to run away, but are captured and killed by the Eragardian soldiers. Soya and the Trio finished off the remaining giants with Theus throwing his hammer at the last one, knocking its head off its shoulders. The hammer returned to Theus as the storm ceased and the moonlight shined upon the melting corpses of the frost giants.

In the distance of the field stood Noldar and Illianna. Noldar, holding his Guilespear, yelled in anger as he witnessed the frost giants' defeat by Theus and the Eragardians. Illianna could only stare at the field, seeing the giants' bodies turning into liquid and melting away into the blood-coated field.

"There will be another time for battle, my lover." Illianna said. "Just be patient with this."

"How can I be patient when the first order of business has failed! Never mind. I will speak to Hadi about this and what is possible."

"You're going to Abaddon?"

"Yes. Where else can I speak with Millennium Goddess of Death?"

Noldar vanished into a portal, going straight for Abaddon. Illianna took one last look at the field, seeing nothing but liquid. She waved her hands and disappeared into a thick green mist. Nowhere to be seen.

Noldar entered Abaddon, the realm of the dead, who are neither honored nor dishonored. He walked through the dark, heated caverns of Abaddon calmly. Aware of the souls that are trapped to endure Abaddon for eternity. He approached the throne room and saw Hadi sitting. He made his way toward her, her two Death-Hounds growled toward him. Standing his guard. Hadi

saw Noldar, commanding the hounds to stay down as
she stood before him. Her tall presence and beautiful
features brought a chill down Noldar's spine.

"So, this is Noldar." Hadi said. "The Millennium
God of Guile."

"Yes, it is I. I am here to receive an audience with you
concerning a troubling matter of my own accord."

"What does this matter of yours have to do with I,
Guile God?"

"I need some assistance with eliminating Theus."

"The Millennium God of Thunder. He's your
problem?"

"Aye. I need great assistance with defeating him so
that I can rule over the land of Eragard."

"For this cause of yours, I surely hope you don't
intend of making a mockery of me."

"I surely do not."

"I'll help you this once." Hadi said, as she waves her
hands toward Noldar. Releasing an aura that surrounds
him and enters his body.

"What just happened?" Noldar asked, looking around
his body, feeling the odd energy.

"When you return to the land of the living, contact
Lordi and Arnos. They will be your assistance in
defeating Theus and conquering Eragard."

"Oh. Thank you, my death goddess." Noldar said.

He proceeded to walk away, but Hadi stopped him.
Turning back to face her, she continued to stare at him

with her dark red eyes, covered with the shadow of death.

"Do your work wisely, Guile God. Because if you do not take heed to your own words, you will end up here with me for eternity."

"I will not disobey."

Noldar left Abaddon through a conjured portal. Hadi sat in her throne. The death-hounds growled as she petted them.

Back at Eragard, Theus traveled to the Asbru, the one-dimensional portal between the fifteen realms. The gatekeeper, Vindhler could hear Theus approaching from behind.

"What brings you here?"

"Just to check on the sources of any other portals popping up around the fields."

"No. No portals so far. But there are some strange occurrences taking place in Eldigard."

"Such as?"

"Gods and heroes of their own. Showing up from the sky before the realm of Man. They're worshipping them as their new gods."

"Should I go down there to check things out?"

"In a matter of time, you will. Just not right now."

Theus nodded. Taking in Vindhler's words closely.

"Well, thanks for your trust and watchfulness,

Vindhler."

Theus left the Asbru as Vindhler continued to keep a lookout into the fifteen realms of Eragard.

II

Noldar returned to his trodden down castle, using the power Hadi had given him to communicate with Lordi and Arnor. He used his portal device to contact them. Letting the power soar through the castle. Illianna entered, seeing Noldar. She ran toward him curiously.

"You're back." Illianna said. "What happened in Abaddon with Hadi?"

"She is willing to aid us in our mission to eliminate Eragard. She gave me this source of power to contact Lordi and Arnor to aid us."

"Very well. After you speak with the two, when do you plan to strike Eragard?"

"Right after I speak with Lordi and Arnor. Immediately after."

Noldar grinned. "No more waiting this time."

A small festival was held at the Eragard Palace with the celebration of the defeat of the frost giants. The people drank and partied as Eden and Meredith discussed plans concerning the realm and what can be done to protect it.

"In time, we will achieve peace in all the fifteen realms." Eden declared.

Theus entered through the scene, walking to his father's throne room. He opened the door seeing Eden inside.

"Father, can I have a word with you?"

"Yes, my son. Of course."

Theus entered the room, facing his father and mother.

"What is it?" Eden said.

"We haven't traced down the source that allowed the frost giants into our realm. We're still looking."

"The enemy will come when he or she decides its necessary. If it is a traitor in our midst, kill them when they present themselves. If it's an outsider, lock them up in the dungeon for future interrogation and judgment."

"I will see to that, father."

The doors shut behind Theus as he left. Walking outside, Soya approached him. He smiled at her presence. Relieved and calm.

"What is it now?"

"We have to find the one responsible for allowing the frost giants here. I sense we know who it is but I can't direct a finger toward him."

"So, it's a "he" that brought the giants in?"

"Yeah. I believe he's closer to us than what we intend to know ourselves. He knows all of us because he's been with us."

Theus began to sense something in the air. It's a heavy feeling. One of great weight. Becoming weary from the sense. Soya noticed him stumbling, as he attempted to stay standing.

"What is it?"

Theus slowly returned to normal. Taking in a breath and wiping the sweat from his forehead.

"A breach has been opened. Lordi and Arnor have been released from their imprisonment."

"Should I get the Trio prepared?!"

"Yes!"

Theus flew back toward the palace. Entering, he returned to the throne room to Eden and Meredith. Opening the doors and standing before them once again.

"You felt it too didn't you?" Eden said. "The tense air entering your body."

"I did. Lordi and Arnor's prison has been breached. They've escaped."

An explosion appeared from the city entrance. At the entrance is Noldar, wearing his dark green and brown armor with his ram-horned helmet. Illianna stood beside him and behind them is Lordi and Arnor. All four prepped and battle-ready. Theus gazed toward the entrance from the palace, seeing them. Soya and the Trio also see them. Theus moved with haste as Soya and the Trio followed him.

"Noldar!"

"What do you need us to do, Theus?" Ornod asked.

"We head straight for them and finish this mess."

Theus flew up into the sky toward the entrance with Soya and the Trio following him from behind as Eden watches onward with Meredith at his side.

They left the palace, heading toward the city entrance. Meanwhile, Noldar, Illianna, Lordi, and Arnor entered the city of Eragard and began slaughtering the those around. Screaming in horror as they're being destroyed. Arnor sliced them with his battle axe as Lordi injected them with a drug, causing them to have deceptive hallucinations and making them believe he's come to protect them. They walked toward him in deception, he snapped their necks one by one.

"Tis' good to be back in the land of Eragard." Lordi gestured. "Wouldn't you agree, Arnor?"

"I do. We can do so much out here to make a statement to all the fifteen realms."

Noldar smiled as he witnessed the carnage unfolded. He turned to Illianna with a bright smile.

"This is the beginning of our salvation, my love! Eragard is ours!"

Thunder roared above them, gaining their focus. Noldar reluctantly glanced up in the air, seeing Theus, Lady Soya, and the Mighty Trio. Illianna looked upward and stared. As did Lordi and Arnos with anger in their eyes. Fire engulfed their insides.

"He's finally come." Noldar said. "The great Theus

Edenson!"

"He brought his whore alongside him, my love."
Illianna said, gesturing toward Soya. "I'll deal with her."

"Noldar!" Theus said. "I should've known you were
behind all of the troubles we've been experiencing."

"Of course, Edenson! Who else could derive such a
plan that would send you and your friends into utter
chaos. Only I, Noldar, the Millennium God of Guile
could do such a thing and all of you know it!"

"End this now, Noldar. Before the consequences
before worse."

Noldar grinned. Loving how his plan is working.

"It will end, Theus. Just not the way you're expecting
it to end."

Lordi and Arnos flew into the air to combat Theus.
Arnos raised his axe, smashing it into Theus, knocking
him down toward the ground. Soya flew toward Illianna
and they engage in combat. Noldar stared at the Trio as
they land on the ground in front of him. Three against
one. Noldar loved those odds.

"Which of you will fall by my hand first?" Noldar
said.

"I'll take the first hit!" Ornod said. "Get ready to fall,
God of Guile!"

Ornod went for the swipe with his battle club toward
Noldar, who made his body transparent, the club swung
through his body. Noldar hardened himself together and
raise his Guilespear, swiping it in the back of Ornod's

head. Knocking him out. He faces the remaining two, Aslan and Vanor, smiling at them.

"Next?" Noldar asked with a big, sinister and happy grin.

On the other side of the city, Illianna and Soya fought, slamming each other into structures. Illianna flew toward Soya, yet, is struck with a right heel, knocking her into a wall.

"You always used your legs for everything." Illianna muttered. "Shame."

"And yet, you're the one who's lying on the ground." Soya said. "Stand up and face me like a woman, witch!"

"With pleasure, whore."

Illianna stood up, snatching Soya by her cape, punching her and threw her into a building. Illianna later controlled some of the nearby people, making them attack Soya. She fought them, but she refused to kill them before she was kicked in the back by Illianna.

Theus is double-teamed by Lordi and Arnos. Using their abilities to pummel him into the ground. They jeered as they proceeded to beat Theus into the ground, deepening him into the ground. A proper burial place.

"You thought we could be kept in a prison?!" Lordi gestured. "You fool!"

"We're Millennium Gods just like you!" Arnos said. "We have power beyond what many comprehend!"

"Yet. You have no trait of intellect nor instinct." Theus said. "Allow me to show you what it truly means to be a Millennium God."

Theus charged up his power within his hands and shoved Lordi and Arnos from him. Through the flying dirt, Theus stood with Mithrandir in hand. He lunged toward Arnos, slamming him with Mithrandir into the ground. Making a quick right turn to swipe Lordi across the city. Theus hovered into the air and released crashing thunderbolts, striking Lordi and Arnos.

"Feel the power of the thunder!" Theus yelled as he released a stronger lightning bolt from Mithrandir, striking Lordi and Arnos.

Noldar began to face Aslan after defeating Vanor with an illusionary attack. While fighting Aslan, Noldar notices Lordi and Arnos have been defeated by Theus. Due to the lightning in the sky.

"No!" Noldar said. "Where's Illianna?! My love, where are you?!"

Upset, he searched for Illianna and saw Soya walking toward him. He can see she's dragging something with her. He looked closer, Soya is dragging an unconscious Illianna. Knowing his plan is failing, Noldar tried to run, but is cornered by a revived Ornod and Vanor. Surrounded by the Trio and Soya, the spark of thunder sounded from above him. He glared up as Theus came down from the sky.

"You got me this time, Edenson." Noldar said somberly.

"You're coming with us. For judgment."

Theus grabbed him, returning to the palace.

Within days, Noldar's judgment took place. Eden had placed Lordi and Arnos into a deeper state of imprisonment. To where neither Millennium God nor gods of any kind could break them out. Illianna had been thrown into a dungeon for a period of a year in the sight of the gods. Eden commanded Noldar be brought up before the Eragardian council.

"By the laws of Eragard, you, Noldar Thanatoson, Millennium God of Mischief and Guile, will be placed into the dungeons of Eragard until the necessary time for your release." Eden said.

The guards entered, snatching Noldar by his arms, pulling him out of the council's sight and to the dungeons. While walking down the alleyway of the dungeon, Noldar looked over at the cells, spotting those who are imprisoned, from trolls to demons to cyclopes to aliens and to Illianna herself.

"We will get out of here, my love." Noldar said. "I promise you!"

He made the attempt to approach her cell and the guards snatched him away from Illianna.

"Keep walking, Guile one."

The guards placed Noldar into his cell and shut the door. Locking it. They walked away as Noldar stared down the alleyway. He hung his head while standing in the middle of the cell. A split second after the guards left the dungeon corners, Noldar smiled.

"I'm inside." Noldar said. "Just as we agreed."

INTO THE WOODS

The US and Canadian Army came into an agreement, ramming through the snow-covered trees of the Boreal Forests of Canada, in search for Kent Brock, a scientist who was caught in amidst of trouble. Soldiers ran amok through the forest, dressed in the appropriate gear concerning the snowy weather. One soldier ran through the forest, surpassing the other soldiers with his speed.

"Our objective is to find Mr. Kent Brock." The soldier said. "Stay on the mission and avoid any distractions that may present themselves."

"Yes sir." The other soldiers replied.

While running in the snowy forest, Kent Brock ran out in front of them in the distance. His clothing torn and worn out, appearing as if he's been on the run for a long time. Clothes dirty and covered in remnants of snow. Kent made the move to run as fast as he could through the snow with his tennis shoes. The snow's feet deepen as he inched further away from the military's presence. Taking a moment to stop, he chose to hide inside a small cave. Running to the cave, he stood by the interior, unseen by the soldiers and jeeps that begin to pass by. He peeked, spotting the soldiers running pass the cave. Kent exhaled a sigh of relief.

"Hope that was it." Brock said.

One soldier inside a jeep saw his radio flickering. He picked it up.

"Yes, General."

"Tell those men out there to find Brock immediately. We don't have much time to waste out here!"

"General, the snow is increasing the further we head into the forest. We can barely get through it with our jeeps right now."

"I don't care how much snow builds up on the damn ground." The General said. "Your direct order is to find Brock and bring him back to base. Understand soldier?"

"Yes sir." The soldier said slowly, obeying the commands of his General.

The radio signal shut off. The soldier placed it into his vest pocket.

The soldier commanded the jeep driver to plow through the increasing snow. The increased speed of the jeeps began to throw the snow into the air, blinding the way for the ground troops and jeeps behind each other.

"We all need to move as fast as we can to avoid being

blinded by the snow!" One soldier yelled out.

Brock still sat by the cave's entrance after the soldiers and jeeps have passed. Taking the moment to calm himself, he started to hear what sounds like a low-pitched growl coming from the deeper region of the cave. He walked into the cave to have a look, to see what it could be, and as Brock took the first step forward a large grizzly bear jumped out in front of him, roaring. Brock stepped back to avoid the bear's swiping of its paw.

"How did a bear get up here?"

The bear continued roaring at Brock as he moved and took steps back from being swiped by the bear. As he stepped back, a group of three soldiers came down from a nearby hill, running through the snow. Through the running, they spotted the cave and saw at the entrance Brock and the bear.

"There he is!" A soldier yelled.

Brock looked over, seeing the soldiers. The soldiers draw their firearms and begin firing at Brock. He ran out of their sight as the bullet hit the walls. The bear ran out of the cave, turning toward the soldiers. Preparing to attack them. They shot at the bear, which continued running through the gunfire. One bullet made its way to the bear, scraping its back leg, causing it to stumble to the ground. The soldiers looked down at the wounded animal.

"Should we kill this thing?"

"No. leave it be. We're not here for it. We're here for

Brock."

They turned around, seeing Brock, who's a near distance from them.

"After him!"

They ran after Brock, chasing him through the forest. One of the soldiers noticed Brock is almost out of their sight, raised up his gun and fired. The bullet flew through the trees, hitting Brock in his left leg. Brock let out a quick yell, falling on the ground and buried in the snow. The soldiers can only track him by searching for Brock's blood within the snow. The soldiers looked further, seeing something shuffling underneath the snow.

"That's probably him."

"Wait one second."

"What is it? We have the fugitive right in our sights. Let's just take him and go back to the base. Leave this white forest."

"What was that the General said about him feeling sharp pains?"

"Something about him transforming. Like a werewolf."

"So, he's a werewolf now?"

"Don't listen to those stories. The General told us that to keep us on edge and to finish the mission."

They approached the shuffling snow and the snow burst into the air with an explosion, shoving the soldiers and knocking them onto the ground. Appalled and slightly frightened, the soldiers stood up and looked toward the snow.

"The hell was that?!"

"It looked like a grenade went off."

"None of us tossed a grenade."

The snow exploded again with a loud, deep roar following. The soldiers remained still as the snow fell from above them like rainfall. Wiping the snow from their faces and off their uniforms, they still stood still. Unsure of what is happening.

"What is that?"

From the snow, slowly rising, was a large figure, covered in gray fur with snow falling from its fur to the ground. The figure stood at about eleven to twelve feet in height. Its long black hair shocked the soldiers oddly as they noticed the torn black pants. Resembling Brock's pants. The soldiers continued to look, spotting the bullet wound on its left leg.

"Shit! That's Brock!"

The figure wiped the remaining snow from its body as it roared. Slowly turning to face the soldiers. The soldiers wait and catch a glimpse of its face. Frightening and terrifying them as they stared into its red eyes, seeing its sharp teeth. The Beast roared at the soldiers and lunged toward them. Snatching one of the soldiers and ripping him in half. The other two try to run away from The Beast, but one falls into the snow.

"Damn it!"

He attempted to get back up, but The Beast jumped

into the air and landed on the soldier. The Beast looked onward toward the third soldier and proceeded to chase him. Roaring as it chased him, trying to reach him. The soldier ran and raised up his gun, shooting at The Beast. The bullets bounced off the Beast's rough, hairy skin underneath the fur. Not having any way to work for him, the soldier pulls out his radio to contact the others, before he could utter a word, The Beast grabs him by the head and throws him into a tree. The forest is now silent as The Beast roars and runs off deeper into the forest.

Only a few miles away from the forest is a set-up military base. The General entered one of the tents and received a radio call from the forest. He picked up the radio.

"News on Brock. Do you have him?"

"No sir. We do not."

"What happened?!"

"Three of us were killed. Brutally killed."

"Return to base now."

"But, Brock sir. He's still out here."

"Turn back now. That's an order!"

"Yes sir. Turning back now."

In the forest, the soldiers signal the others, commanding them to turn back. They went ahead and left the forest without any other explanation given to them. Inside the base tent, the General looked at a map of Canada. He drew a line on the map, starting from Manitoba to Toronto to the forest.

"Where are you headed?" The General uttered.

<u>THE SUPREME ENCHANTER</u>

A young woman ran toward a small shack in the cold and wintry forests near the area of Nepal. She moved with haste, not bothering to make a simple stop or slow down near others who were in her way. She stopped at the shack door and knocked three consecutive times. No answer. She knocked again and no answer. She continued to knock until the interior lock clicked. She took some steps back from the door as it opened, revealing a man dressed in black clothing with a cloak and tunic. His facial hair stood out with his emerald colored eyes locked onto her.

"Why are you so far out here, Madame?" The man asked.

"Are you who they say you are?"

"Pardon?"

"Are you the Doctor?"

"Which doctor? There are many of them around

these lands."

"Doctor Donald Fortune. Is that your name?"

"It is. Why have you come to my assistance, lady?"

"I need help. It's an urgent matter and I want them gone."

"Want what gone?"

"These demons. They continue to mock me about my past experiences. I can't take their voices no longer. I've heard you can cast them out."

"I've cast out devils in my time of service. I'm not sure if you understand the cost of what could happen to you when the casting takes its place."

"I don't care. I just want them gone. Out of my head, so I can have a full conscience. A clear mind that I can control."

Fortune nodded. Allowing the woman to enter his shack. Closing the door, she looked around Fortune's shack, seeing artifacts that pertain to mysticism and spiritualism. From his cloaks to his staff, which is said to have belonged to a powerful wizard during the early middle ages. His name unknown to the world, but known to Fortune and others like him. She went to touch the staff slowly with her finger.

"I suggest you keep your hands to yourself while you stand in here." Fortune said. "You have no idea as to the amount of power is withheld inside that staff."

"Sorry."

Fortune poured the woman some hot tea—which she

drank, sitting down at the table in front of him. Fortune examined the woman, from head to toe. Searching her spirit through his mind. Within her, buried deep are the demons. Laughing and mocking her and her past actions. Fortune can hear the conversation between the demons. Their laughter itches Fortune—he starts to slightly rub his arms to remove the aura from his body.

"I can hear them." Fortune said.

"What?" The woman said, putting the tea cup down. "What can you hear?"

"I can hear them within your being. The demons. They're laughing and mocking you. Speaking of your past experiences as if it's only a show to them. They enjoy seeing you suffer from those moments and they relish it with all their power."

"Can you remove them?!"

"I can."

Fortune stood up from the table and walked into the middle of the shack. His hand extended out toward the woman. Looking at her eyes with caution as he can see the demons starting to manifest within her.

"I need to know if you are ready?"

"I am."

"Then come. Lay down on the floor and I will begin the casting out process."

The woman walked to the middle of the shack. Fortune removing the carpet, revealing a painted pentagram on the wooden floor. The woman jolted for a moment—seeing the symbol on the floor. She stood still, shaking and holding herself still. Fortune looked at her and knew it was the demons making their move to hold her back from the floor. She and the demons were playing a spiritual tug of war and Fortune could sense which side was winning.

"You'll have to be strong and fight against them. Only then will you make it towards the floor. Be strong and fight them within."

The woman struggled making her way towards the floor. She took several steps and the growls of the demons could be heard through her own voice. Fortune stood calm, awaiting to see the outcome of her determined will to lay down atop the pentagram. Fortune aided her with words, throwing out positive suggestions to give her internal strength to continue fighting the demons.

"Keep going, lady." Fortune said. "You're almost there."

She struggled constantly, slamming herself on the floor. The demons went silent as she looked around, seeing Fortune standing over her. He smiled and walked to the other side of the pentagram. Standing in front of her feet—Fortune grabbed and put on his other cloak. Different from the last one; a violet one and within the cloak was the Amulet of Quirinto, a mystical object filled with great power and vast knowledge used for such situations. Fortune stood in front of the woman as she looked up at him. His arms stretched out and his eyes closed. Standing next to him was a podium. Atop the podium was a grimoire which had the title of *'The Book of Durriken'* written on its cover.

"By the power of Quirinto, I bind the demons within the body of this young woman and command them to come out immediately!"

The woman began to scream as if she was in tremendous pain. The pain a woman would feel during labor. Fortune sensed and knew the screams were from the demons making their anger known from within her. She shook around on the floor, trying to stand up, but the mystical power of Fortune's enchantment held her down as if she was tied to the floor. Fortune continued to chant out the words to cast out the demons. Their screams had increased in both pitch and sound. From around her arose a cloud of black smoke and within the smoke were the demons themselves, hovering over her and staring at Fortune. Their eyes flashing from within the smoke and Fortune could only smile.

"You." The demons said in conjunction.

"Yes." Fortune said smiling. "It is me. I know of your kind. You're all soldiers, aren't you?"

"We do what our Master requires of us!"

"I can tell you do and your mission has been halted. You can blame me and my knowledge of the mystical."

"You play around with such power and use it on weaklings like this woman! You have no true knowledge of what great power is. Our Master will find you and he will end you!"

"Be that whoever your Master is, give him a message for me. If you will so, please."

Fortune raised his hands and appeared a glowing blue aura—which surrounded the demons and started pulling them into the pentagram. Fighting the pull, the demons screamed at Fortune, scratching and clawing at the woman to hold on. Finding themselves becoming transparent and losing their grip as they were almost pulled into the pentagram completely. One demon had raised its head up and roared at Fortune with a deep glare. Fortune looked in the eyes of the demon and laughed in its presence.

"We will find you and we will destroy you!" The demon declared with a deep pitched voice.

"You may try demon." Fortune said. "But, I am no ordinary man. I am the Supreme Enchanter and by the power of Quirinto through the Mystic Father, I now banish all of you back to your wicked kingdom! NOW!"

A powerful gust of wind blew throughout the shack, blowing the demons through the pentagram and within a split second—the demons were gone. The woman's eyes had opened, she slowly sat up from the floor. Looking around the shack, only see Fortune kneeling in front of her.

"How do you feel?" Fortune said.

"I feel… I feel clear." The woman responded with a

smile on her face.

The woman stood up from the ground and thanked Fortune. A few minutes later, she walked out of the shack, smiling and full of happiness. She turned around to Fortune and hugged him.

"Thank you, sir."

"One more thing before you go, Madame."

"What is that?"

"Do not repeat the same actions as before. For if you do them, the demons will return with more than what was before and more aggressive in nature."

The woman nodded with a slight hint of fear in her being.

"I understand."

"You don't have to fear them." Fortune said. "Do not repeat those actions and you will be fine."

The woman nodded, thanking him again for his help and she waved goodbye to Fortune. Fortune entered his shack and closed the door. He sat down at his table, raised up his cup of tea and took a sip. He released a slight sigh.

A NIGHT IN LOS ANGELES

The streets of Los Angeles, California are crowded with pedestrians and police as they stand in front of a bank, waiting for the robber to walk out with the bags. The news stations arrived and are making the broadcast live throughout the city. Inside the bank, the robbers hold a stand-down against the bankers and the civilians inside. Few of the bankers held their ground and faced the bankers off with firearms of their own.

"I've always wondered if you guys carried heat." One robber said.

"Few of us do." The banker said. "Now, put down the bag with the city's money and walk out of here. Turn yourselves in to the police. Do yourself some good."

The robbers laughed as they pointed their guns toward the bankers. Their laughter ceased into silence.

"Nothing funny around here but us leaving with the money." The second robber said. "How about that, tough guy."

Inside of a room, sat down Steve Walker, who watched the live feed broadcast of the bank robbery. He looked around the area, seeing the amount of people standing out in front of the bank and the police with their guns in hand.

"The police won't be able to handle all of that on their own." Steve said. "I can take care of their problem."

Steve walked toward his closet, opening the doors, he kneeled toward the floor and pulled out a case, which when he opened it, released a small shock. Steve smiled when he looked inside the case.

"Let's do this." Steve said.

The robbers are slowly taking steps toward the exit of the bank with the bags of money in their hands. Their guns still pointed at the bankers.

"You two won't get away with this." The banker said.

"What does it look like we're doing, dumbass." The robber replied. "We're getting away."

The robbers opened the front doors of the bank, slowly walking out. As they turn around to the street, they see the pedestrians and police facing them. The police held their guns tightly aimed on the two robbers. Both robbers smiled as they backed up against the wall of the bank.

"Put down the bags and get on the ground now." A policeman said over a megaphone. "I will not repeat myself. Put the bags down and get down."

The robbers looked at each other and gazed their eyes

around the pedestrians and back to the police. They both nodded and put down the bags. They slowly went down on their knees as the other police surrounded them.

"Do it now." The first robber said.

Both robbers jumped up and from their sides, shot out a small machine gun, which they fired at the policemen and the pedestrians. The pedestrians and policemen ran for cover to avoid being shot by the two robbers, who laughed and cackled at the sight of the people's fear. The machine gun fired with immense speed for its small size.

"Now, this is what we came here for!" The second robber said.

"You got that right, friend."

The robbers continued to shoot at the police and the scattering pedestrians covering the streets and surrounding areas. The robbers kept up their laughter of excitement as the machine gun fired at its quick speed. Instantly, within a flash of light, the machine gun stopped. The robbers both paused and glanced at their guns, seeing them destroyed with a hole burnt through them. Catching them off their guard.

"What just happened?"

"You tell me! Something shot right through our guns man. Burnt them up."

From the sky, the sound of cackling was heard as the two robbers gazed up and witnessed a lightning bolt coming down from the bank and onto the pavement in front of them, between them and the police and pedestrians. From the lightning bolt emerged a man who was wearing a uniform that covered his entire body from head to toe. The colors of the uniform were blue with yellow lightning bolts on his arms and lower body with his upper body to his head in yellow with white eyes and a red V on his chest made from lightning bolts.

"Who the hell are you supposed to be?" The robber said.

"Yeah. What are you? Lightning-Man?"

"Well, Lightning-Man seems kind of lame. But, I'll tell you my name after you return that money back to the bank and surrender yourselves."

"As if!"

"Suit yourselves, gentlemen. Prepare to get the ass-whooping of your lives."

The robbers pulled out handguns from their sides and began to shoot at the uniformed one. The robbers fired constantly, and the uniformed man jumped up into the air, dodging the bullets, which appeared to him to move in slow-motion at the increase of his speed. The robbers started to show frustration, seeing their shots aren't hitting the man as he moved through the air in quick speed. Appears as a lightning bolt to the people standing on the road.

"What is this guy made of?!" The robber said.

"I don't know but he's moving at a speed where we can't keep up!"

The man landed on the ground, causing the robbers to cease their guns and stare at him. The police and pedestrians have no idea to make of what they're witnessing. The uniformed one began laughing at the robbers, cracking jokes about their knowledge of using guns. The robbers, now angry run toward him to which he jumped up and flipped over the two robbers, kicking them in their faces. The man laughed as he leaned against the bank wall.

"Is this all you two have?"

"We have more than that!"

The robbers ran to harm him, but he dodged the attacks, causing the robbers to punch each other in the process. He kicked them in their chest, knocking them to the bank wall. The uniformed one turned toward them and started shooting lightning bolts from his hands. The lightning bolts created a net of static electricity, holding the robbers against the bank wall to where they couldn't make a move. The uniformed man grabbed the bags of money and approached the police. Placing the bags on the ground in front of them.

"Here's the money and my job here is done."

"Sir, we appreciate the assistant, but what should we call you?"

"You can call me The Voltage."

The Voltage raised his arm up, firing a lightning bolt into the air, which he grabbed onto and was gone in a bolt of light, streaking across the night sky over Los

Angeles. The next day, the news featured a report speaking of the robbers being placed in the Los Angeles jail and how the city is giving thanks to The Voltage. The city is embracing him and have given him the full title of The Astonishing Voltage.

THE BATTLE OF THE KINGS

I

The underwater city of Atlantis is being attacked by a group of Sea-stormers, all swimming toward the throne room. They carry with them swords, shields, and spears. Crying out a chant toward their master. Within the walls of Atlantis, the Atlantean army is prepared for the battle that awaits them outside. Behind them walks out into the room, their leader, Kular The Aqua-Barbarian, also the King of Atlantis. He gazes toward the outside, seeing the sea-stormers approaching. Kular busted through the throne doors, swiping the stormers as they came. More Atlantean soldiers appeared from the upper layer and fought alongside their king. Taking out the sea-stormers as quickly as they possibly could.

"Who are they lead by, my lord?" An Atlantean soldier said.

"Those belong to Sea Kaiser." Kular said. "He seeks to take the throne. He will learn not to threaten the true

King of Atlantis."

Kular made the move to bring his army ahead, as he could see a swarm of sea-stormers making their way toward Atlantis. In front of them was Sea Kaiser. Fully prepared for war in his scaled-spiked armor. His helmet resembled a crab mixed with a spider. His dark silver cape flowing with the currents of the sea. His eyes shined red as blood through the waters. In is right hand was a trident of his own with five points. He raised up the trident and pointed it toward Atlantis.

"My legion. This will be the day you will tell your descendants. The day where I conquered the kingdom of Atlantis and rid its place of the line of Kular.

Kaiser moved through the waters with such speed, he was far from his army. The sea-stormers moved in packs with their swords and axes in hand. They chanted the name of Sea Kaiser as they approached the gates of Atlantis. Kular waited for them to arrive. His army was set to battle the stormers. Kular's eyes were glued to Kaiser. Both kings. Each seeks ruler ship over Atlantis, yet, only one can be called king.

"They're inching closer, my king."

"Let them make their way inside." Kular proclaimed. "Once they're in our circle, we can handle them swiftly."

Kaiser blasted a lightning bolt through the gates, allowing his army to enter. They entered Atlantis with a screeching yell and they collided with the Atlantean soldiers. Fighting amongst teach other in the deep waters of the sea clashing swords against axes and shields against spears. The golden armor of the soldiers bolting with the silvery armor of the stormers. Kaiser moved past the soldiers' battle and went directly toward Kular. Both wielded tridents in hand.

"You know what must be done today." Kaiser said.

"Your nonsense comes to an end." Kular replied. "That is what must be done this day."

"I will only cease my actions when I'm dead and food for the critters."

"You've forced my hand to make it so."

Kular and Kaiser clashed their tridents against one another. Shoving the other back a few feet before running toward each other and clashing the tridents together. They held their weapon tightly in a tug-of-war scenario. Showing who had the most strength. Strength in their mindset fit for a true king. Kaiser's red eyes glimmered over Kular's pale eyes. Neither blinked.

"You know this is where your reign ends." Kaiser mocked. "Just accept it and hand me the keys to the kingdom."

"The keys? How would someone such as you wield them with your self-righteousness and arrogance."

"You'll see if I keep you alive."

Kaiser kicked Kular in the right leg and tripped him onto the ground. The currents of the sea increased, interrupting the ongoing battle between them. Kaiser didn't mind the movement of nature and continued to attack Kular. Slamming his trident against Kular's rough skin. The impact only felt like a bat was being slammed into Kular's back. Kular arose and punched Kaiser, cracking a side of his cowl, tearing off once of the spider-like features.

"How dare you ruin such a crown."

"It's not a crown, Kaiser." Kular pointed. "It is just your covered hatred for yourself."

"I will not hear any more of your treacherous words!"

Kaiser went to collide with Kular and quickly, the sound of a trumpet was blown. Kaiser turned around to see an arsenal of Atlantean soldiers. Equipped with weapons and beasts of the sea. From sharks to whales to lobsters. Kaiser knew what was about to unfold. He turned around toward Kular.

"Stormers! Out!" Kaiser yelled. Signaling with the waving of his right hand.

The stormers evaded the kingdom. Leaving at such a quick rate. Kaiser followed them, and he turned, pointing at Kular with his trident.

"This is not over between us."

"I am aware." Kular replied as Kaiser left with his army.

Kular took a moment and checked his army. Few were dead from the battle and they were buried in the undersea cave and a small memorial was held for them.

Kular returned to his throne room as Kara of Atlantis appeared before him. Kular loved the presence of his wife after a battle. Her long silver hair gave him hope. Her blue eyes he cherished. Her beautiful countenance subdued his rage. Kara is no stranger to the art of war. Whether it be against friend or foe. The scars on her arms and chest as pure signs of her time in war.

"I'm sorry I didn't attend the battle."

"It was of no need. Kaiser decided to pick such a moment to face me. You saw how he ran once you and the reinforcements had arrived."

"You told me you needed them just in case of another major war. Now, that I've returned, I see another war is imminent and it's with Kaiser."

"It will be over within the moments the sun rises and the moon sets."

Kara sat next to Kular at the throne. She rubbed his shoulders, feeling the only scars of war. Kular's body is covered with them. Kara can sympathize with Kular's experience in the heat of battle. Both are prone to having a desire for combat and a lust for rage. Kular was comforted by Kara's presence. She kissed him and led him into their chambers where they had their fill of love for the remainder of the day into the night.

Kular arose from his bed the following day. Filled with more energy than the day before. He walked out of his chamber and headed for his study. Upon entering the study, Kular was met with the presence of his advisor,

Novah. Novah bowed before his king and Kular gesture waved it off.

"There's no need for that." Kular said. "You knew me before I became king."

"That is true. However, I came into your study to give you a few words of wisdom. I'm sure you'll want to hear them."

"Always. What is it you have learned?"

"I believe Kaiser's attacks will not cease. Nor will his desire to usurp the throne of the kingdom from your severed head. I figured by now, there's only one way to deal with Kaiser and his sea-stormers."

"And what is that?" Kular wondered.

"You must kill Kaiser. Once you do so, his stormers will immediacy give their loyalty to you and you will have both armies at your disposal. For whatever cause may come upon Atlantis in the times to come."

Kular took the time to walk around his study. Thinking on Novah's words. The advisor watched his king take the walk. He could sense the mediation and the fighting of the mind in Kular.

"Not to rush your judgment, you will need to make a choice sooner than later. We both know Kaiser will not wait another day to return and repeat what he did yesterday. By now, he's probably already only a few miles out from the gates."

"You know I and Kaiser grew up together. We're like brothers. Attached in the art of war. We bonded together due to war."

"I know. I was there by your sides with your father when he was king. I saw what you and Kaiser had become. A powerful unit against the enemies of this kingdom. Only then, when your father had passed, and the crowd was given to you did Kaiser change his motives and he ran. Went into the deeper layers of the seas to gain answers."

"And he did. Explains where the stormers came from. We didn't deal with those kinds of soldiers when my father was king."

Novah approached Kular and placed his hand on his shoulder. Kular nodded with respect as did Novah.

"Just be quick with the decision." Novah said. "Not hasty."

Novah left the study with Kular alone. He sat down at his desk, staring at a map of the seas. The map decorated with kingdoms and tribes across the world. Atlantis wasn't the only kingdom in the seas. Something most of the surface world has yet to learn. Kular's mind was on planning and it might cost him.

II

Kular exited his study to find Novah. He approached him nearby the inner aquarium of the palace. The walls covered in crystal coral intertwined with the branches of the sea trees. Novah turned toward Kular.

"What have you decided, my lord?"

"We're taking the fight to Kaiser and his stormers. End all of this for good."

Novah nodded with a smile. He was certain of his king and couldn't agree with a better choice.

"I'll rally the army." Novah walked away.

Kular returned to his chambers to find Kara awoke and dressed. He told her of his decision and she was trusted in it. Both walked out toward the throne room where they were met with the entire Atlantean army and Novah standing before them. Kular nodded.

"For Atlantis."

Kular sent out a beacon toward Kaiser, who sat out in the distant miles within the walls of an ancient destroyed castle. A castle once home to another great king of the seas whose name has been hidden by time. Kaiser saw the beacon echoing through the waters and he arose. He walked out of the castle with his stormers following. They saw the beacon and as it began to light up as red as fire. Kaiser grinned.

"You're growing a pair. Finally."

The sea-stormers rallied together, bulked up in their

armor. Clashing their weapons together to spark the blood through them with Kaiser delivering to them a speech of war. They shouted out a war cry as they moved toward the kingdom. Meanwhile, Kara pulled Kular aside with Novah. They decided possible scenarios of an outcome. Kular's only scenario was to stop Kaiser from his continuing invasions. Novah stated he wanted Kaiser dead, and Kara couldn't agree more. They believe with Kaiser dead, Atlantis would sit better under the seas.

"If I were to kill him, it would only alarm the others roaming out there to come here and try the same."

"Then let them come." Novah declared. "And when they do, they shall suffer the same fate that awaits Kaiser and his stormers."

"I agree wholehearted with Novah, my love."

"I can see that." Kular nodded. "We'll see what today brings us."

The sounds of horns sounded from afar, gaining their attention. They looked out and in the watery fields they saw Kaiser and his stormers moving fast. The swam quickly toward Atlantis and the stormers began firing electric beams at the gates, blasting them open. Kaiser relished the scene of the falling gates. His hopes were high this day, believing Kular has set himself up for good. They shoved their way into the kingdom and instantly the battle was taking place.

Kular and Kaiser clashed with their tridents. Both fought vigorously. While fighting, Kular noticed Kara taking out several of the stormers. He was impressed, and her fighting style turned him on. He caught himself and continued to focus on Kaiser who was slamming his trident against his own.

"Getting distracted?" Kaiser noted.

"Doesn't appear to seem the case." Kular said with a punch to Kaiser's cowl.

Novah watched the battle from within the palace. The number of soldiers fighting one another was massive. It covered most of the seabed and Novah sat down at a table facing the battle and he pulled out a scroll and began to write. Kara grabbed one of the staves of the stormers and used it against them. She saw a handle on the staff and pressed it, firing a blast of electric bolts at the stormers. She paused and smiled.

"We could use something like this."

Kular and Kaiser's fight reached the interior of the palace with the two bleeding from the nose and mouth. Kular dropped his trident and Kaiser understood the purpose. He dropped his and the two kings fought hand-to-hand. Kular delivering punches and haymakers, breaking Kaiser's cowl once more. This time, the cowl fell off to reveal Kaiser's true face. A scarred one, yet his blue eyes glowed in the waters.

"Removing who I am doesn't stop the fight."

"That's not why I did such a thing. I did it to reveal to your stormers who you really are."

Kaiser rammed toward Kular, spearing him to the

ground. He punched Kular several times in the face and he loved it. Kular knew it and rolled Kaiser over on his back, smashing his face with his forearm. Kaiser laid on the floor of the palace, laughing. Mocking Kular for his fighting. Kular arose from the floor as Kara entered the palace. Novah sat at the table above them, overlooking.

"You're finished, Kaiser." Kular declared.

"I'm still breathing. If I can breathe, our war will never end."

"Don't make me do it."

"You have no other choice, Kular. It's the only way."

Kular nodded and grabbed is trident. He held it as Kaiser stood up on the floor. Kular paused and saw Kaiser standing still. His arms held outward. His chest boasted forward. Novah saw the actions and he could only think of one thing. Kara stayed quiet while seeing Kular making his decision.

"This is the only way!" Kaiser yelled.

From behind the Atlantean army and the stormers entered the palace and watched. Kaiser looked at his army and he could sense what was about to happen. It didn't concern him, and he continued to yell at Kular to kill him. Kular gave him a stare. A stare of hope.

"I'm sorry." Kular said. He rammed his trident through Kaiser's chest.

Kaiser took his final breaths and fell to the ground as Kular lowered the trident. Kaiser laid on the ground motionless and the stormers stood still. Kular and Kara faced them, seeing Kaiser's army kneeling before him. Novah was astounded as he continued to write on the scroll. The armies cheered Kular's victory and Kara sealed it with a kiss. Novah smiled and rolled up the scroll.

Days later, Novah spoke with Kular about the aftermath of the battle now named, "*The Battle of the Kings*". Kular stated he didn't want to kill Kaiser and felt the conviction that it was the only choice. Novah later told him after searching through the archives and studying the maps in the study, the other kingdoms of the seas have learned of Kaiser's demise and are already preparing to attack Atlantis. Kular was ready for the incoming kings and queens. But before the wars for the seas would begin, Kular set himself a clock with a visit to the surface world. He heard about the rising heroes appearing across the world and he figured it was time he went out there and saw them for himself. Maybe they could be of help in the future.

<u>QUANTUM MISSION</u>

Isaac Edison prepared himself for a night he would hopefully forget. Only if it went wrong. Isaac, a well-trained scientist still in his twenties who's hope relies on his technology that will enable a wearer of the tested uniform to shrink or grow their body size depending on the right numbers associated with the wearer. His first test mission was to infiltrate his competition's headquarters. The name of the competition was JarvisTech. The owner, Jarvis Tesla is a famous scientist and technician. Primarily, the feud between Edison and Tesla resembles the old rivalry of Thomas Edison and Nikola Tesla. Only if they switched places.

Isaac arrived at the JarvisTech headquarters later in the night to avoid major security. Even though, the surroundings of the interior were crawling with suited gunmen, Isaac geared himself up in his designed suit. Putting on the leather suit coated with Kevlar, he was covered in shiny silver with remnants of dark blue pouring out from the angles. His eyes were as blue as the deep sea. His flesh was hidden by the suit's detailed features and Isaac snuck into the headquarters through one of the first-floor windows.

"Ah." Isaac muttered to himself.

He moved as quietly as he could through the hallways to avoid the armed security. They moved through the building like ants delivering the food to the anthill. Isaac made his way toward the laboratory of the headquarters. Within the lab, were prototype suits like his own. Isaac warned Jarvis about developing suits like his own to avoid confusion amongst the public and to keep the suspicion of a military presence away from their work. Jarvis had other plans and sought out to lure the military toward his company and to enlist himself in developing the suits for the soldiers to wear during warfare. Isaac desired to keep his creations away from the military's hands and from the fields of war.

Isaac entered the laboratory and the first thing that caught his eyes were the suits. Detailed in black with gold lining. Like his own, only the coloring was different. Isaac felt ashamed of Jarvis' plans for military use. He noticed there were gauntlets on the sleeves of the suits. He recognized them before when he once visited a military base and saw their weaponry. The things they're capable of that are hidden from the public.

"Now, to find a way to shrink these things." Isaac said, staring at the line of suits.

Isaac extended his arm toward the suits after taking a few steps back. He continually gazed toward the door, waiting for the security to come bursting in and shooting him. The area was silent, and Isaac focused his sights back onto the suits. The gauntlet on his wrist wasn't designed for weapons-use. He fired it at the suits and within a split second, the suits were miniaturized. Isaac yelled in his helmet at the sight. The yell echoed out into the hallway, catching the attention of one security guard.

"Shit."

He gathered the miniature suits, placing them in his pocket. He could hear the footsteps approaching the laboratory doors. He nodded and pressed a button on the gauntlet of his sleeve and the doors had opened. The security guard entered the levorotatory and saw no one. He nodded and left the lab. On the floor stood Isaac, the size of a penny.

"That was a close one."

Isaac set himself to escape the headquarters. Upon doing so, he exited the lab to find himself surrounded by three security guards. Their guns aimed toward him. He nodded with a chuckle mumbling in the helmet. The guards were tightly noticed. Their hands gripped their firearms steady.

"Remove the helmet." One guard demanded.

"I don't think that's a good idea, my friend."

"We're not your friends, thief. Remove the helmet."

"Can't we just talk this through?" Isaac asked. "Like adults?"

Isaac sighed. He waved his hand toward them and reached for the helmet. While reaching, he moved his hands close tighter and quickly tapped the gauntlet button, shrinking himself before their eyes. The guards stumbled at their feet. Looking around the floor for Isaac.

"The hell did he go?"

Isaac arose from the floor in normal size knocking the guards out in succession. They fired their guns at him and his shrinking avoided the fire. His strength increased by the size-alterations. After taking the guards out, the alarms went out through the building, allowing Isaac to make his escape.

The following day, Jarvis entered the headquarters with his high posture and fast-paced walk to learn of the events that transpired the night before. He rubbed his head and removed the button from his suit. Enraged of hearing about a helmeted man sneaking into his lab and discovering his suits were gone. He decided to pay a visit to Isaac's laboratory. Driving toward the lab, his phone rang, and he answered.

"Hello."

"Sorry to bother you, Jarvis. It's me Isaac."

Jarvis sighed with anger in his throat.

"You understand I'm coming to pay you a visit."

"For what reason?"

"Don't play around with me. I know it was you who infiltrated my laboratory last night and stole my suits."

"I didn't technically steal your suits. I took them to see what you'll do if they happened to have gone."

"Now you know. You're just the same as before. Young and foolish."

"I don't see how."

"Those suits are for the military. They need gear like that in the heat of battle. Standard soldier suits aren't a match for the technology they face daily."

"Designing those suits for war will only cost you more than your company. You need to leave it be and focus on better things, Jarvis. Things that can save lives."

"War saves lives, Isaac. But, you're just too arrogant to understand that kind of cost."

"When you get here, your suits will be ready for pickup."

"You better not have altered them, or I will strangle you with my hands."

"The suits are well. I haven't done anything to them that would harm your reputation or the feats they are capable of."

Jarvis nodded. "Good."

In his lab, Isaac read up on the details regarding the incident from the previous night. He gazed over to his suit with the label, "Atom-Zero" listed above the helmet. He laughed to himself as his phone rang. He looked at the ID and it read, "Michelle". He nodded.

"Guess I have to take this."

He pressed the phone to answer. Exhaling very slowly. Michelle is one of Isaac's close partners and she doesn't take kindly to his kind of methods when it comes to learning about the competition and their work.

"Yes ma'am."

"I heard about what happened last night."

"It was just a mission. Call it a quantum mission."

"You understand Jarvis will be coming for you, right?"

Isaac gazed over toward the Atom-Zero suit and smirked.

"I'll be ready."

CHASER OF SOULS

"We have to go!" He shouted. "We must leave!"

The man shouted continually as he witnessed his partner raping a young woman in an alleyway of an urban city. His partner relished in his actions. Shaking his head, he grabbed his partner by the shoulder, pulling him away from the woman.

"Didn't you hear what I said! We need to go. Now."

"Come on." His partner replied. "Why do we need to go? There's no cops nearby. Nonetheless anyone else near this alley besides the two of us and this hot spice here."

He glanced down at the woman, who's crying from the incident. The partner grinned. Loving her cries.

"Besides, I'm not done with her just yet."

"You're not listening to me."

"Why should I by the choice of your words, partner?"

"Because he's coming."

"Who's coming?"

"The one who collects the souls of the sinners."

"The what?" The partner questioned confusingly. "Who's coming?"

"The one who chases after the souls of sinners."

"You're talking about Jesus?"

"No. I'm talking about someone else. Something else."

The partner refused to believe him and went back to raping the young woman. He goes to pull his partner from her once again, by the touch of his hand to shoulder, the partner backhands him, knocking him to the ground.

"Let me have my fun!" His partner yelled angrily. "I want to enjoy this night."

The partner returned to the woman as his teammate arose from the ground. As he stood, watching he looked across the alley and saw what appeared to be a man. But it was not a man. He could tell by its eyes and the presence. He started to back away, seeing the entity coming toward them.

"He's here!" He yelled. "He's here!"

"Shut your mouth!" His partner replied. "Leave me be with your superstitious talk."

He ran from his partner and out of the alley. His partner looked up, sensing someone standing near him. Believing it to be his partner.

"I told you to lea-" He said before gazing the eyes of the Death Chaser. His head covered with a hood and his leather-type clothing standing out. Spikes on his shoulders and forearms. his eyes glowing with a burning fire. The essence of fear stroked the partner immediately.

"I have come for you." The Chaser declared. "Let the woman be."

The partner stepped back from the woman, who ran. The Chaser took small steps toward the partner as he began to plead for his life.

"Look, I was only looking for a good time. Not much was happening tonight."

"You do not know the deed you have done. You have deflowered a virgin. One that could've reach a great price to a worthy man."

The Chaser snatched the partner and rammed him against the wall. He held his head tightly as he screamed out for mercy.

"You want mercy from me?"

"Please! I'll go home, and I will forget this moment ever happened! I won't bother any other woman like this ever again!"

"I will give you mercy."

The Chaser stared his eyes, measuring his spirit. The Chaser nodded and stared at the partner.

"What are you doing?" The partner asked fearfully.

"Very well. I have searched the reins of your heart. Therefore, I declare you need the Cry of Repentance."

"The what?"

The Chaser breathed on the partner, endowing him

with the memories and the pain of the actions he's committed, including the recent act done to the virgin. The partner yelled in pain, falling to the ground as the Chaser overlooked him.

"You are in pain." The Chaser said. "For the moment. Afterward, may you have learned you lesson. If not, I will return for you and that moment will be your final day on this Earth."

The Chaser walked away, vanishing through the dim light as if he was a physical ghost. The partner continued yelling in pain. Begging for help. No one came to his aid and he remained in the alley until the morning when he was found by police and taken to the hospital. There, it was seared into his mind, he met the Death Chaser, the Soul of Retribution and Chaser of Souls.

THE PURPOSE OF DARKNESS AND LIGHT

A group of untrained wizards meet up in secret within the bowels of a undisclosed location. Although, it's near a forest, not known which forest it could be. The wizards have agreed to meet up together to conjure up an entity of any kind to prove to their doubters that they are real wizards in the flesh.

"Are you sure we'll be unseen from this place?"

"I have to ask the same thing. What if that "swordsman" guy shows up and sees what we're doing here. He might toss us into Pegasus for all we know."

"What if that guy from Enigma City appears in the sky over us? If he shows up, we're as good as dead."

"No one is showing up to stop us. The only thing that will make itself known is what we conjure up from our ritual."

The leading wizard creates the surrounding landscape

they will set up the ritual and the location for the entity to conjure out of the other dimensions before them. The wizards are prepared for anything to take place as the other two are in fear of who will show up during their ritual.

"Shall we begin."

"Yes." The wizards said. "Let us begin."

The leading wizard begins to recite a spell from a scroll, kept within his robe. Reading from the scroll, the area stars to shroud up with strange smoke. A dark smoke with a bluish hue to its appearance. The leading wizard continues reading, the language is Latin.

"*Vobis hodie vocamus, olim domini de adumbration! Alterum nobis cum surrexerit Sabaoth!*"

The ground vanishes around the wizards. They can't even see the ground through the dense smoke. The Wizard continues chanting from the scroll and they hear footsteps approaching them. Coming within a distance. The wizards shiver in fear and in excitement. Waiting for their master to make himself known unto their presence.

"Please greet us!" The wizard shouted. "We need your eyes to gaze upon us!"

Through the smoke appears a figure. Standing tall over the wizards. They crouched down to their knees, bowing before the shadow figure as it walks toward them and through the smoke. The smoke doesn't even make a touch to the figure's body as it flows through the figure. The wizards take notice and believe their master has come. The figure stood before them, gazing down at them with its white pupils.

"You have summoned me from my home." The figure declared.

"Yes. Yes, we have."

"For what purpose to you disturb me?"

"We desire to have your powers." The leading wizard said. "With your powers, we can change this world for the better. Get rid of all these folktale figures popping up across the earth."

"You believe you can do a better job than those who are already doing the work?"

"Yes, master. We surely believe that fact."

The figure nodded, and the wizards bowed their heads.

"Very well." The figure said. "Take heed of the words that I'm about to speak to you."

"Yes, Master. We will."

The figure raised his arms above hem and into the night sky. The wizards gazed upward, seeing before them one side of the sky covered in the darkness of the night and the other side shining in the brightness of the day. The leading wizard became confused by the message in the sky.

"What is this sign you've given us, Master? What does it all mean?"

"You seek to have the powers of the darkness. To do your work upon the earth. Yet, you have no knowledge of the light. How can you control the darkness without the intellect of the light? It is a shame for your kind to have such feats."

"You can teach us this mighty works. Please, teach us the things you can do, and we will grow in them and we will achieve our mission."

"I will not teach you these things you have seen this night."

"Why not?! We summoned you hear to give us knowledge of the shadows. To do things which no other humans could possibly comprehend."

"Yet, none of you can comprehend what the signs of the sky declared before you."

The figure waved its arm, removing all the smoke from the area. Clearing it out completely. The wizards took cover as the gust of wind blew away the smoke. After the gust settled, the wizards raised their heads up toward the figure and the could see it and they were frightened. More frightened than when it first appeared.

"You're not our master." the leading wizard said.

"I am not." The figure replied.

"Then, who are you? Who are you that can create the signs of the sky and reveal those feats before us?"

The figure stood before them closer. Revealing his true form. His form was of a pale man with long black hair and black facial hair. Dressed in all black, with a black trench coat, shining with the hints of royal violet. His eyes completely black with his white pupils shining from them. The wind blew around him slowly while snippets of thick darkness surrounded his presence.

"I am the Keeper of the Cosmos. I am Darkous of the Astrals."

"The Astrals. They can't be real."

"You're looking at one now and we are all real."

"Then, what will you do to us?" The leading wizard asked. "What could we have possibly done wrong this day to insult a true Astral entity?"

"Go home." Darkous declared. "Return there and leave this life of the mystic arts."

"Leave it?"

"Yes. Leave this life. Live a life such as a human should. You're not fit for this purpose."

"What purpose?"

Darkous turned away from the wizards, preparing to leave them. The leading wizard stood up and ran toward Darkous. Reaching out with his hand, he touched Darkous' coat. Darkous stopped and turned toward the wizard.

"What purpose?!"

"The purpose of darkness and light."

Darkous' pupils turned from white to red and within seconds a flash of light bolted from him. Blinding the wizards. They ran around, searching for the wall to lean on and while they were doing such–Darkous was gone. Nowhere to be found.

ARROW FOR HIRE

"Take the shot. Make it count."

The Hitman was steady in his shot. He laid atop the cold ground in the desert. It was nightfall and his rifle aimed toward a mansion. A part was taking place within the residence and the Hitman couldn't be glad to deliver his gift to their cause. The target was standing before him. Inches away. He took the shot and killed his target. Those surrounding the target fled to save their lives as the Hitman gathered his equipment and left the area. The news of the Hitman's attack went across Las Vegas and reached Asher Dale—one of the city's most profound businessmen and philanthropist.

"Excuse me, Mr. Dale. Have you heard about the incident regarding the death of your former competition last night?"

"I did, and I can assure you, I had nothing to do with his death. Our quarrel was strictly business-related."

From across the room, Karen Harp approached Asher with a tight hug. The two are close friends and business partners regarding city business. Those around Asher aren't keen on getting any closer since the attack.

"You know what happened last night?"

"I've been hearing about it all day." Asher said. "Trust me, I had nothing to do with it."

"They're already putting you on the suspect list."

"Why? We were only enemies in business. We only had disagreements. That's all. None that would make either of us plot to kill one another."

"I know you and I know you wouldn't do such a thing."

"So, you believe me?"

"Of course, I do." Karen said with sincerity. "It's just how you're going to convince everyone else."

Karen took a quick glance at her watch.

"I have to go. I'll see you later."

"Sure thing."

Asher returned to his office where he's greeted by Carvis Hoyt, his assistant and mentor. An older man full of experience in the field of combat. Carvis heard about the attack and decided to speak to Asher concerning its matter and the implications he had placed on Asher's shoulders. Carvis could discern the weight on Asher's shoulders due to the those who are looking at him as the prime suspect.

"I know what you're going to say." Asher said.

"Do you?"

"Eh… somewhat."

"This Hitman that's come into the city. Do you have an idea who he might be?"

"Not exactly. I can pinpoint some possible suspects. But, it won't be enough to figure out who he may be."

"Or she."

Asher gave Carvis a look of confusion. The look didn't bother him, only gave him a little more insight that he was able to put in Asher's mind. Carvis nodded with a smile.

"You've seen what people are capable of doing. Anyone could be this Hitman."

"I have." Asher sighed. "Maybe I can call in a few friends of mine. See what they think of this issue."

"No need. They have their own business to deal with This matter is in your hands, Asher."

"Fair enough."

Asher sat in his office for most of the day, reading up on many sources that are possible traces to the Hitman. Later in the afternoon, Asher left his office and returned to his home. Inside the home, Asher prepared himself for the night to come. Removing a large box from the closet and he opened it. Inside was a dark golden suit. Covered with Kevlar. Also laying in the box was a golden bow and a quiver, full of arrows.

"Here we go again." Asher chuckled.

Night has fallen when Asher met with Carvis in his

hideout. Carvis read up on all the Hitman's possible activities in Las Vegas and handed the details over to Asher. Asher, fully dressed and hooded in his gear approached Carvis who reacted with a slight twist of the head.

"What is it?"

"You'll always make me second-guess myself when you're wearing that thing."

"What's wrong with it?"

"Maybe a little too much gold for my taste. Should've been black or brown."

"No offense, they were already taken. Besides, gold fits my personality."

"Tell me about it." Carvis laughed.

Asher glanced at the files and noticed a strange similarity between the Hitman's last kill and his forthcoming strike. Asher searched on the computer sitting at the desk and learned of the Hitman's next possible targets. A real estate agent, a hotel owner, and a police chief.

"Three choices and only one to focus on." Asher said.

"Which do you think this Hitman will strike first?"

Asher glanced to the information of each of the three possible targets. Reading up on their details and learning of their current whereabouts in the city, he headed out to meet all three of them just in case of a possible strike. Asher went out and confronted the real estate agent. Learning there was no one in sight. He made his next move toward the police chief, discovering the chief was far out of the city for the day. Asher move in haste to find the hotel owner and learned the owner was sitting in one of the hotels in downtown Vegas. Asher entered the office of the owner, entering through the window and terrifying the owner.

"Sorry about this." Asher said. "You have to get to safety."

"Why?"

"That Hitman is coming for you."

"Why me?"

"I don't know. But, you need to get to safety now. Do you have a place of security in this hotel?"

"I might have."

"Get there now and wait for my signal to come out."

The owner ran to leave the office and within an instant a gunshot speared through the window, hitting the owner in the back. The owner felt to the floor with Asher ducking down and crawling toward him. Asher rolled him over, only to see the owner is dead. Asher sighed slowly and rose up toward the window. He looked and what he could see was the light reflecting from the scope of the Hitman's rifle. Asher jumped from the window, running over toward the Hitman.

"Don't move!" Asher said, pointing an arrow toward him.

"I won't." The Hitman said. "It's about time we meet."

"Guess it's not what you had in mind."

"Oh no. this is what I wanted. I came to this city to confront you."

"You killed two people only to get me out here?"

"Yes. How else would I grant you a moment of your time?"

"Why are you in Las Vegas? Your true purpose?"

"I'm here to give you an offer. One you can't refuse."

"What kind of offer?" Asher asked, his hand steady on the bow and arrow.

"Kill me and rid this city of anymore sudden deaths."

"You're asking me to kill you?"

"Yes."

"There's something else with this. I can sense it in your voice. What's the catch?"

"The catch is really simple. Once you kill me, you will become the killer. Henceforth, the new Hitman of Las Vegas."

"No." Asher nodded slowly. "I won't kill you. Not for your own gain."

"Then expect more people to end up dead."

The Hitman raised up his rifle and Asher fired the arrow, hitting the Hitman in his arm. He ran over and slammed the bow across the Hitman's head, knocking him out. Asher sighed and took a moment to breathe.

"You're crazy." Asher muttered.

Asher had delivered the Hitman to the Las Vegas Police Department where they took him in for questioning. Carvis confronted Asher back at the hideout where he was stocking up on new arrows.

"I heard about the Hitman."

"There's something more going on with him." Asher said. "Something I clearly have no understanding of."

"Such as?"

"He wanted to be caught. He wanted me to bring him to the authorities and I don't know why."

"What could it be for?"

"Maybe the offer he gave me."

"Offer?"

"He wants me to take his place as the Hitman of the city. I turned him down."

"I've never heard of such a deal before. We have to keep an eye on him."

"I have it covered."

Asher pressed a button on the keyboard, revealing a camera in the interrogation room where he and Carvis could see the Hitman being questioned. The Hitman was sitting calm. Neither was he shaking or trying to escape. He looked as if he was right at home. It shook Asher's mind to see the Hitman in such a state.

"He doesn't look to be in any sense of fear."

"He's not afraid. He's in a good mood."

"I don't like this."

"Neither do I."

"Now, what is your plan concerning this guy?"

"I don't know."

"What if he escapes suddenly? How will we deal with him? A Hitman on the loose in Las Vegas."

"I'll have it covered. Trust me."

Carvis nodded with certainty. Asher nodded back and Carvis left the hideout. Asher continued to watch the camera feed. The Hitman only told the officer the same answer repeatedly.

"The Q-Arrow brought me here and he will set me free."

THE AVAGO LAND

A pair of travelers rode a shore toward an undisturbed and unsearched island near the Atlantic Ocean off the coast of Africa. The island appeared to be a simple one. Typical in nature. Massive trees and filled with animals. The travelers coming toward the island were four in number.

"This place could possess treasure." One traveler said.

"Are you sure?"

"Can you just be positive. At least this once."

"Once we find some valuable, I'll be positive."

The leading traveler, Eric had spoken to the other travelers about the island and what he's heard of it from those who lived in its surroundings. Mostly those who live on the African coast.

"What did those people tell you about this place again?"

"They said there's treasure here." Eric replied. "Lots of

it. Never been touched by anyone. Ever."

"They told you that?"

"Yes, they did. What of it?"

"Nothing." He said. "Just I find it strange they would tell you such things without being here first."

"Maybe they're afraid."

"Afraid of what?"

"Whatever could be living here."

The ground began to tremor. Eric and his group can feel the small tremors beneath them. The tremors move one after another. Like a continuing beat of a drum. Birds flew out of the trees in haste, startling the group.

"What is going on?" Eric wondered.

The tremors increased, and they could hear something rushing through the trees. Cracking and rustling could be heard from around their location.

"What's happening, Eric?"

"I. I have no idea."

The sound of the tremors grew and from the trees bolted out a large Tyrannosaurus Rex. The T-Rex released a mighty roar, terrifying the group and Eric. They made a run for it with the T-Rex chasing them.

"It's a T-Rex, Eric!" One group member yelled. "A T-Rex!"

"I know!" Eric yelled back. "I know!"

The quaking sound of the T-Rex's footsteps increased the terror and dread within the group and Eric along with them. Running toward another end to enter into the trees, they hastily jumped, and the T-Rex made its attempt to burst through the trees. Yet, the trees were too thick with branches for the creature to enter. The T-Rex roared into the trees and walked off. Eric and the group arose on the ground, covered in bushes and small broken branches.

"Is it gone?"

"Yeah." Eric said. "It's gone now."

Preparing themselves for another solution and plan, the tress around them begin to move and the continuing sound of cracking branches is increasing near them. They stood together in a circle, looking at every angle. Terrified, they all pulled out weapons to defend themselves. Eric was the only one with a firearm and everyone else had either a knife or some type of blade.

"What is that?"

"Just stay quiet." Eric commanded.

From the trees around them appeared slowly a tribe. Startling them for a moment, they gazed toward the tribe who were covered in symbols unknown to Eric and his group.

"We're not here to harm anyone." Eric said to the tribe cautiously. "We're only here to search for treasure and artifacts. That is all."

The tribe surround Eric and the group and split themselves apart. Unknown to the group, walking out of the forest is a man with a saber-toothed liger at his side. Eric paused as did the group, seeing the man approach them. he was muscular in form and his long brown hair intrigued them. He looked different than any of the tribesmen and women. He wore plates of a strange armor on his forearms and legs. Few of the plates were worn on his chest.

"You're not from here, are you?" Eric asked the man.

The liger growled toward Eric, pushing him several steps back into the group. The man approached Eric and the group with a slight calm. He stared at them, measuring them up.

"You've come for treasure?" the man asked Eric.

"You... You speak our language?" Eric asked with peaked interest. "Yes, we've come searching for treasure."

"You cannot have what is ours." The man declared. "Leave this place. Never return."

"What?" Eric said. "We cannot just leave this place. We need to bring something back with us. To civilization."

"I care not for your world." The man said, staring at Eric. "You've invaded my home and you want to take what is valuable with you."

"Valuable? What do you mean by valuable?"

Eric questioned and looked again at his armor. The metal was unlike any mineral known to modern man. It appeared to look like any other metal, but its texture and its shine made it stand out from the rest.

"You speak of your armor." Eric pointed. "That isn't any ordinary metal you have."

"It belongs to me and to the people of this land."

"Listen, you could give us a little trinket of that metal and we'll be on our way."

"No."

"Why not? You could be sitting on something that could change the world as we know it." Eric said, his voice determined he wanted the metal by any means if it came to it.

"I care not for your world."

"Look at us and look at you." Eric said. "You're not like the tribes' people. You're one of us. You belong with the modern civilization."

"I belong here."

"Have you ever heard of a cell phone? Internet?"

"They have no interest here."

"Eric, I think we should just leave." said one of the members.

"Please, I'm begging you. Give us a little bit of the metal and we'll leave your home. For good."

The man paused, he looked once more upon Eric. Seeing his smile and his seriousness of gaining the metal. The man looked toward the others of the group and could see their stillness of fear. They feared him and the tribes people.

"I'll give you something."

"Oh. Thank you. I hoped you would come around-"

The man raised up his blade and sliced the throat of Eric. The group yelled in panic, seeing Eric slowly fall to the ground as the man stood over him and the tribes people inched closer.

"You wanted the metal." The man said to Eric as he gasped and choked on his blood.

Eric died choking on his own blood. The blade was made of the same metal worn by the man. The group was in terror as the man stared at them, placing the blade into his sheath on his leg.

"We didn't come to cause trouble."

"So, I can sense." The man said. "Leave this land. Keep your lives."

The group ran out of the forest, leaving Eric's dead body on the ground as the saber-toothed liger snatched the body, dragging it into the forest. While the group left the island, they looked out and could see the man watching them leave with the tribes' people standing around him. They knew they would never forget their journey into the Avago Land.

CHICAGO'S GUARDIAN

"I saw him."

"Saw who?"

A police detective asked an eye-witness to a crime. The eye-witness was terrified not by the crime, but by what saved her from the crime's ongoing havoc. What she is describing to the detective is something the detective who assume to be a fantasy.

"You'll going to have to give me more details as to what you saw, ma'am."

"I'm telling you what I saw. It was a figure with horns. It was dark red, it had red eyes. they glowed. I was afraid."

"But, this figure didn't harm you. It saved you from the attacker."

"Yes. That is what's frightening me even more. I would've thought it would have just killed me and the criminal. Not just the criminal and letting me live."

"Are you positive it wasn't just some guy in a red coat. maybe it was this "John Terror" guy the city keeps hearing about. Maybe he decided to have a change in attire for once."

"It wasn't him. I'm aware of his insignia. The man I saw, he had no insignia. It was just the dark red and the horns. And the eyes. Those glaring eyes."

The detective sighed. Putting down his notepad on the desk. He leaned in toward the witness who was still shaken by the crime scene and the sighting of the figure with the horns. He reached for her hands and she reached over to him. He held her hands calmly to settle her mind and body. The witness began to calm down.

"We'll do what we can to find this figure." The Detective confirmed. "But, for right now, it's best you return home and leave this to us. We'll find out for sure."

"So, there's no need to put me in witness protection?"

"No reason to. You aren't being tracked down by some criminal. You were saved from a criminal. It's better than the other possibility."

The witness understood and was taken home by a fellow officer. The detective gathered the information given to him by the witness on the horned figure. The detective entered another office. The office was packed with files. One drawer was labeled, "Outside Cases". The detective opened the drawer and within it were other detailed sightings of the same figure with minor sightings of the John Terror individual.

"Where do these things come from?" The detective asked himself.

After the hours had passed, the detective left the station. Upon reaching his car, he felt the need to gaze up toward the sky. As he looked up, he saw the tall buildings of the city and atop of one of the buildings, he could make out the shape of a figure. Standing still. As if it was a statue made into the building's structure.

"The hell?"

Squinting his eyes to have a better look of the figure. He could make out the dark red of the figure's body and the horns on its head. The detective reached out for his phone and began taking quick photos. After snapping continually photos, the figure had vanished. The detective put down the phone to see the figure had left. He entered his car and began looking at the photos taken. On several of the pictures, the figure was blurred out. Only two of the photos feature a clear look at the figure. One where the figure is standing upright and the other with the figure crouching down. He could perfectly make out the dark red colors, the horns, and the eyes. Exactly how the witness described the one who saved her earlier that night.

"She wasn't lying."

The detective drove off from the station with only one thing on his mind. The city of Chicago has yet another guardian.

ALLEY BRAWL

In the evenings, there would be fights, and the fights would include many who have proclaimed the streets of Boston, Massachusetts as their own. The fights were set up in clubs. Packs to determine which group would maintain control over Boston's streets. In the fights would be former bouncers of the city's night clubs and street gang members from all the parts around. Usually, the fights would have them nearing a defeat by knockout. Others were sometimes critically injured and killed in the fights.

The fights are illegal according to the state laws. During one of the late-night fights, one fighter stood out as a proclaimed master of throwing fists. He defeated over several men and stated his purpose was to take over Boston with his fighting style. To recruit others into his fold and to train them as he has learned himself. He returned daily to the fights and participated. He came out of every fight as the victor. After each victory, he gained one member for his gang. With the new of the rising heroes coming across the streets of Boston with one hero nearby in New Jersey, the man decided he can't hesitate to take a chance at confronting one of the heroes.

After a period, and more fights won, the man had himself a gang of his own. With this power, he sent out a calling card to any of the rising heroes across the United States to meet him in Boston at the fights. Starting he will face them one-on-one in a fist fight. He declared if the hero won, he would cease participating in the fights. However, if he won, the hero must denounce themselves from their newfound calling. Days had passed and not a single word was returned to the man. Weeks went by and there was only silence on his end. It wasn't until a month had passed with two men walked down the alleyways of Boston toward the fights.

They were different than those who had come before. They each had their own distinctive appearances and styles to their attire. One had black hair cut short with facial hair and blue eyes. He wore only black jeans and a vest. He wore white wristbands. The other had red hair down to his shoulders and red pupils, wearing a dark red vest with black leather pants. On his chest was a torso tattoo of a sword engulfed in flames. They approached the fight scene and through there, the man and his gang turned their attention towards the two men.

"Might as I who are the two of you?" The man wondered.

"Me and my friend received word about fights happening in this particular area and we've come to discuss terms."

"Discuss terms? Of what kind?"

"You called out these 'rising heroes'." The man with the red hair proclaimed. "We're here to accept your challenge."

The man and his ganged mocked the two men. Preferably their dress and their words. They couldn't take them to be actual heroes. Their laughter didn't bother the two men as they appeared to have known it would happen amongst those in the gangs and clubs.

"There's no need to make up lies."

"What lies have we to offer other than your supposed victory over one of us."

"You're both serious about my offer?"

"Why else would we be here?"

"Understood." The man said. "Before I defeat one of you, what are your names. So that I can spread them across the city and later the country to your shame?"

"I'm Jack Stone."

"And the one with the red hair?"

"Dante Hale."

"Jack Stone and Dante Hale." The man gestured with a smile. "What kind of names are those? Did your mothers give the two of you those names or did you change them because of some troubled past?"

"No need of your concern." Stone said. "Are you ready to fight?"

"So, you're going to fight me? Why not your fiery friend?"

"Trust me, you wouldn't want to face me in a fist fight."

"Besides, he's more skilled when it comes to swords."

"The hell." The man questioned to himself.

"Step into the circle, Mr. Stone."

Jack Stone stood in the circle, being surrounded by the crowds cheering on the man for his past victories. Stone scoffed at the crowd before facing the man. He was ready for the fight and gestured some taunts toward Stone.

"We never got your name." Stone said. "Mind if you tell us?"

"My people call me Mark Jensen. Head of the Crossbones of Boston."

"We're on good terms then."

Jensen circled Stone as the crowd cheered continually. Dante Hale stood against the brick wall of the alley way, watching the fight and shaking his head. He foreknew what Jensen had got himself into and was only waiting for him to find out.

Jensen ran toward Stone with right hooks and jabs to the abdomen. Stone was unfazed by the hits. Jensen continued to attack as the crowd started to dim down the noise. Jensen paused himself, realizing his attacks did no harm to Stone and Stone only smiled.

"They didn't even leave a mark in your flesh." Jensen said. "Not possible."

There were no marks on Stone's body. His skin didn't even turn red or any color from Jensen's quick and strong punches. The crowd was amazed at Stone's body. They were shaken and were worried. Jensen himself was unclear to why his attacks didn't bulge Stone's body. Stone punched Jensen and by the punch, Jensen was knocked out cold. The crowd backed away from Stone and Dante approached him. They looked down at Jensen and shook their heads.

"Damn shame it had to go this way." Stone said.

"He knew was he was in for." Dante mentioned. "To a degree."

Stone turned toward the crowd, spotting out Jensen's gang standing around him and Dante. They weren't going to attack because if they did, they would turn out like their leader. Stone stood before them with his hands open and his arms out.

"When your leader wakes up, tell him to turn over to a new leaf. The East Coast Alliance will be handling this around here from now on."

Stone and Dante left the alley way as the crowd tried to return to its now ruined evening. Jensen's gang stood over their leader, waiting for him to awake. They took one more look at Stone and Dante as they left from the alley way and they were clear to remember what Stone had told them concerning the East Coast Alliance.

THE SLY DETECTIVE

The night sky covered the city of London. Its landscapes brightened by the light. Within a warehouse owned by several politicians, a group of armed men formed in cargo gear and faces covered with masks entered and they carried boxes. Cargo boxes in pairs of four. Walking into the warehouse, the guards were certain their business would go smoothly that night. Only then did the lights flicker and illuminate continually.

"What's wrong with the lights?" One had asked. Glaring at the lights with confusion.

"Probably didn't pay the bill."

"Doesn't sound like something they'll forget. Especially with this deal of ours."

They laid the boxes across the floor in a single-file line. The armed men believed their business was done and the lights had bolted apart. Complete darkness filled the warehouse and the men were prepared. Their rifles were aimed steady across the warehouse. They scanned above themselves and in front of themselves. They were certain whatever may have caused the outage wouldn't last any longer with their firearms up and ready.

In the darkness, the only sound that could be heard was the pummeling of fist to body and fist to head. The clapping of rifles touching the ground echoed through the warehouse and the remaining men began firing their weapons. Through the flashing in the darkness, they could make out an image attacking them. It was of a woman cloaked in a trench coat, dressed in all black. She even wore a black hat as she fought each of them with only her fists and boots.

The lights returned to their former state, revealing the armed men on the ground. Knocked inconspicuous. Only one of the men remained in his awareness state as he backed up against the wall, seeing the one who attacked his partners. He felt ashamed it was a woman who took them out, but her strength proved to be nothing else but supernatural. To his mindset. The woman approached him as the sound of her heels clapping against the floor gave him a shake in his body. She reached out and grabbed the man by his throat, pulling him closer toward her face. He glared into her eyes and could only feel a shivering fear within him.

"Who's responsible for this deal?" She asked.

"I… I can't tell you."

"Why not?!"

"Because, if I do, they'll do me a lot more harm that what you've done to my partners."

"Your partners won't have to suffer the same fate you will if you refuse to give me the names I am asking for."

"Who are you anyway?" The armed man asked with confusion. "We've never encountered a woman like you who could take out as many men on your own. Only with your hands and feet."

"I'm what you can consider a change in the world. You've heard of the rising heroes. I am one of them."

"You don't say? I thought they were all fairy tales. You know. Like Snow White and the Seven Dwarves."

"You believe them to be only tales read to children before their bedtime? You have so much to learn about the true world we live in."

The woman snatched the man's army, twisting it as he screamed in pain. Her strength terrified him even more feeling his arm almost to its breaking point. He continued to scream as she waited several seconds for him to take in the pain.

"The names."

"I'll give you one. One is all I can do."

"Why only one when you can give me all of them?"

"Because, the name I know should be enough for whatever it is you're searching for."

She twisted his arm once more before letting it go. The man panted in pain, holding his right arm as she stood over him. Her presence had begun to scare him even more than her skills. Her countenance hadn't changed since she entered the warehouse. She was focused solely on her purpose.

"Good thing it isn't broken." The man gestured.

"Keep silent and it will end up broken. Maybe your other arm will too."

"What? Why?!"

"Give me what I've asked for and you will be spared of having two broken arms."

"Alright. Alright. The name that I heard over the comms before we headed out here was Anne."

"Anne?" She asked harshly.

"Yes. The name is Anne."

"Do you know where I can find this "Anne"?" She demanded after nodding.

"I'm afraid not. They don't tell us where they're located out of fear for circumstances like this."

"Oh. So, they do fear something. That's good to hear."

"Please, let me-" The man said before the woman placed her foot on his chest, shoving him against the wall.

"Why would I let you leave while your friends are having their rest?"

"I gave you what I know!"

"And I'll have to deal with it. That still doesn't give me the idea of letting you go. The police will come here and see what remains. You'll be here to answer their flowing questions."

"Why me?"

"Because you're still awake and in pain."

The woman stomped his left leg and he screamed with a loud yell. Grabbing a hold of his calf and he held it tightly as the woman began to leave the warehouse. He watched her as she climbed the top of the warehouse, walking near the upper windows.

"Who are you anyway? Your name?"

"You want to know my name?" She asked. "Why?"

"That way I can find you later."

She laughed under her breath and stared at the man in pain. She nodded with a gesture of her fedora hat.

"I'm one of the figures from those fairy tales."

"Which one?"

"Should be obvious to a Londoner."

The woman grappled her way out of the warehouse almost like a bolt of lightning had moved through the upper layer of the building.

"The hell is happening." The man said to himself, holding his arm and leg.

Not long after the incident, the police arrived after receiving an anonymous call and closed off the warehouse. They questioned the man and he gave every detail he could about what had happened and the woman he encountered. The officers were already aware of the strange woman. They've been searching for her ever since she appeared in London following the rise of crime activity. The man had asked them if she had a name and all they could give him is the name, *"Cinderella"*.

WELCOME TO T.I.T.A.N.

Max Martin ran toward his home after a day at school. Max Martin is one of the top in his class. Grades are the most impressive amongst those in his rank. He's received college scholarships from many colleges across the country. Max noticed several black vehicles parked in front of his home. He wondered and was curious.

"Those aren't family cars." He said. Brushing back his scruffy hair.

Upon entering his home, he found his mother and father sitting in the living room on the couch. Unsure as to why they're not making any movements. Marx continued walking and sees his parents sitting with men dressed in all black. Their uniforms mimicked the military. One many came from the hallway, staring at Max.

"What's going on?" Max asked.

"We need to have a talk with you, Max."

"Why me? What have I or my parents done wrong?"

"Nothing." The man said. "We're here on good terms. Nothing bad will happen to you or your parents. You can trust me."

"How can I be sure of your word?"

"Sit next to them and I'll explain everything you and your parents need to hear.

Max sat next to his parents on the couch. Removing his red jacket and laying it across the couch's head. His backpack sat on the floor in front of his feet. The man from the hallway sat down in front of him and the parents while the other men stood by the windows and door. Scouting as if they were watching for someone else to arrive.

"What I'm doing here, and my men is of great detail."

"You haven't told us anything." Max's mother said. "Please, we want to know what's going on? Why have we been targeted?"

"Why, ma'am? Because of your son's great feats."

"Is this some kind of internship?" Max asked. "I'm only wondering because it sounds like one."

"It's not a college internship. Yet, it's close to one in detail and function."

"Then, why is my son a great concern to you?" Max's father wondered.

"His intellect requires him to be of service for a greater cause. A cause that will enable him to fully adapt his feats into a greater work. Not just a work to preserve a city or a people. But, the earth itself and perhaps the universe down the line."

"The universe?" Max jumped. "I don't think I can help the universe. I'm just a boy."

"Who will soon become a man. Your future is looking to be glorious, Mr. Martin."

"Then, why do you want our son for your work? What benefit will it do you?"

"He will benefit us greatly and more profound. He will benefit himself and those he cares about."

"What is this 'internship' of yours?" Max asked. "Is it some facility like a science laboratory or a medical center?"

"A combination of both and other details." The man said. "It is a global organization that watches out for those who can't protect themselves from greater threats."

"What threats?" Max's father asked. "Like terrorist threats?"

"Something along those lines."

"Is this some military organization? Our son is not joining the military."

"This isn't the military as you know it. Anyhow, your son would suit better in other areas that do not pertain to the battlefield. We already have a team operating on those terms and it's going about well."

"What is all of this for really?" Max asked. "I just want to know so I can continue on with my life."

The man smiled and pointed at Max. the parents

even wanted to know what was going on and who the man worked with and for.

"My name is Colonel Evan Nader." He said. "I am the Operating Director for T.I.T.A.N."

"T.I.T.A.N.?" The parents said together.

"I've only read small paragraphs about an organization with that name." Max said. "I've seen them in class on rare occasions. I read what they do and what they work with. I thought it was a bunch of rumors made by folks on social media."

"They're not rumors, Max. They're real. Whatever you saw on the internet pertaining to us, it has some truth to it. Lots of truth to it."

"And this organization deals with?" Max's mother wondered with seriousness.

"Espionage and cryptozoology. Nowadays, we deal with those called the rising heroes or the rising figures. Some are human. Others nubreeds and bio-organisms. They exist and live amongst us. You might have some as neighbors around here and don't even know it. That's how the world is today, and it will continue to grow as the years go by."

"You want me to join you in this?" Max asked. "In all of it?"

"Yes. Your skill set requires us to have you. We haven't come across anyone else in years who can do what you can."

Max turned to his parents.

"Maybe I can go along with him and learn things about the world."

"We're not going to send you off with a stranger to an unknown place." Max's father said. "We're not doing that."

"The place isn't unknown." Evan declared. "We have been watching your family for some time now. How else would we know where to come and what time to pay you a visit? Right before he left school and entered this home. This was all pre-planned from the beginning. It was bound to happen as we saw fit."

"How much time do I have to make a decision?" Max asked.

"As long as you need. We're not going to force you to come along with us. You have a choice to make and it is up to you alone to do so. Your future requires it."

Max nodded, he talked it out with his parents in front of Evan. He listened to their conversation until his phone rang. He stood up and walked outside with two of his men as Max continued speaking with his parents. Both parents were uncomfortable with Max leaving with Evan and, yet Max knew it was his decision and he came to one. Evan entered the home after his call and sat down in front of the Martin family.

"Have you made a decision?"

"I have." Max said. "I'll go along with you."

"Understood." Evan said. "But, when?"

"What?"

"I can sense it in your voice. You're not leaving with us right now. So, I ask you, when?"

"Can you give me the weekend? I want to spend some time with my parents before I go."

Evan nodded with a smile. "Of course."

Evan stood up and shook Max's hand. Evan also shook the hands of Max's parents. No matter how much they continued to tremble.

"We'll be in touch."

Evan went to leave after his men had exited the home. He turned back, seeing Max walking toward the hallway.

"Max Martin." Evan said.

Max turned around to face Evan.

"Welcome to T.I.T.A.N." Evan said.

Max nodded with a faint smile and went to his room and Evan left the home. Outside, the black vehicles drove off the property as Max Martin prepared himself for a complete life changing experience that he's about to possess.

THE ABANDONED HOTEL

During the early fall season and with heavy snowfall, Travis Vail traveled past Vancouver, Canada, heading towards an abandoned hotel named The Black Raven. The hotel is known for its prestigious setting as well as its number of floors. The floors of the hotel are a total of thirteen floors and all of them have a large majority of haunting that witnesses have suspected to be spiritual and demonic occurrences, some have even been attacked by the unseen forces.

Vail arrived at the Black Raven Hotel and found no one there but himself. While walking closer to the front entrance of the abandoned hotel, he heard a vehicle approaching him from behind. He took a turn around to see the vehicle and its driver. The vehicle parked next to his and the driver exited.

"I do not know who you are or where you come from, but you cannot enter this place." The driver said.

"Why shouldn't I enter?" Vail said. "Is it because of the spirits?"

"Yes sir. I'm giving you a fair warning here. I heard that some guy was going to go inside the place and try to contact those things in there. You make a mistake, you could release them out here."

"Judging by the way you speak, you do not understand the spiritual realm nor its duties." Vail said. "You are speaking with the Spirit-Seeker and there aren't many as I in this field. So, please do me a favor and return to your home in peace and leave the spirits to me."

Vail turned away from the driver and approached the hotel entrance doors. The driver, filled with emotions, ran over toward Vail and snatched him by his right arm, trying to pull him away from the doors.

"You need to leave this place, sir!" The driver said. "It is not safe to be here at this particular time and season!"

"Unhand me or I will suggest placing you inside this hotel and you can deal with those who are unseen to the human eyes."

"You wouldn't do that to me. I'm just an ordinary guy. I have a job, I have a wife, children, a home, a car. I have a life. I'm just trying to get you to understand that you must save yours before you make a mistake."

Vail stared at the driver and smiled.

"As always. Men like you aren't truly built for what awaits you after this life you're currently living in. Men like you will never fully awaken to understand what lies behind the scales that cover your sight. You and people like you are blinded to the truth and you never seek to find it nor the ones who hide it. Therefore, you are wasting your time trying to change my ways because I've already chosen my path as it presented itself before me."

"You must not enter this place! You cannot! Its suicide!"

"Suicide is what you do when you've given up your belief and strength in things beyond your comprehension."

Vail snatched his arm back from the driver and approached the hotel doors. He placed his hand on the door handles and pulled them back toward him. The hotel doors swung open as if a gust of wind had blown out of the hotel and into the open area. The driver panicked and ran to his car, screaming for his life.

"You've opened the doors! You've released the spirits!"

The driver pulled back and drove away as Vail watched him leave and gave a slight smirk.

"Now, let us see who's waiting for me in here."

Vail walked into the hotel and looked at its interior lobby area. Vail took a few more steps into the lobby area, the two entrance doors shut as if someone had closed them from the inside. Vail looked back and circled the lobby.

"I fully understand that there are thirteen floors in this place and I intend to search them all before the night is fully over. I hope those of you in this place can and will understand that."

Vail walked by an elevator, knowing there was no electricity operating inside the hotel since its abandonment. Vail walked past the elevator and as he approached the end of the hallway toward the staircase, a small bell rang behind him. Vail turned back and sees the elevator light blinking.

"Interesting and intriguing."

Vail walked back toward the elevator and the doors opened as if it was set up for him to enter. Vail nodded and entered the elevator. The door shut and the elevator operations as if it was still in use. The elevator goes up and stopped at the second floor, the door opened, and Vail exited the elevator.

"I take it that someone is on my side in this place."

Vail found himself in the hallway of the second floor and all that surrounded him are the rooms and the equipment which was left behind before its closing. He walked through most of the hotel searching for any signs of spirits. Not finding anything related to the spirits in the rooms on the second floor, Vail went toward the staircase door and the elevator dinged again. Vail turned toward the elevator and its door opened once more. Vail chuckled as he entered.

"Third floor I take it."

The elevator moved up and stopped. Its door opened, allowing Vail to step onto the third floor of the hotel.

Vail stepped out and felt a gust of wind move past him. Vail quickly turned to his right and saw a shroud of mist hovering through the hallway, entering a room without the door being opened.

"Here we go."

Vail ran toward the room door and opened it. He gazed around and doesn't spot the mist which flew into the room, although he can hear what appeared to be people talking amongst themselves in the hallway, which doesn't startle him, but raised his awareness of his surroundings.

"There's more of you on this floor I take it. Proves very interesting."

Vail stepped out into the hallway and could still hear the voices speaking to each other as if they were having a conversation to themselves. Vail reached into his coat pocket and pulled out the book of rituals. He raised the book up above his head and circled in his steps.

"You see this book I hold above me, spirits? This book will send you into the Other Side, where you all will be judged for your actions here on earth and will prove your eternal place."

A form of wind began to pick up from inside the hallway, Vail continued to speak toward the voices and held the book above his head. Vail continued as he saw shady forms of humans, all appeared to be yelling at him in anger and hatred. Vail knew these kinds of spirits and raised his voice as he spoke to them.

"I will not repeat myself to you spirits of the demonic darkness!" Vail said loudly. "You will respond to me and you will enter the Other Side and be judged for your earthly account."

The spirits screamed toward Vail as each of them began to fly toward him and entered the wall behind him. Vail never flinched when the spirits flew pass him. He continued to speak to them and held the book continuously above his head.

Vail understood a few of the spirits had indeed went over to the Other Side while the remaining ones had decided to remain in the hotel in order to attack Vail in any shape they could.

"I know you've traveled to the upper levels of this hotel, spirits. I intend greatly to seek you out and to release you from this place you currently call your home."

Vail walked toward the elevator and it no longer worked. Vail shrugged his shoulders, taking the stairs up to the fourth floor. Upon arriving on the fourth floor, Vail didn't receive any communication or sound from a spirit of any kind. He searched every room on the floor to make sure there wasn't a spirit hiding amongst his presence.

"Fourth floor appears to be clean." Vail said as he checked the last room.

He went up into the fifth floor and all he could see around him was trash and left-over furniture sitting out in the hallway. The hallway had an odor resembling a dumpster, which would be sitting out back or on the side of the hotel, though there were no dumpsters near the hotel. Vail searched every room on the fifth floor, jumping over rugged and molded furniture to get into some rooms. Some of the rooms had a damp feeling and they possessed the smell of damp air after a rainfall.

"Fifth floor is clean. Spiritually clean I might add."

Vail arrived on the sixth floor and as soon as he took a step forward, a mist of cold air blew past him. He could feel the presence of a spirit, whether it be human or demonic. Vail smirked as he walked slowly down the hallway, which was much cleaner than the fifth floor.

"Finally, one of you has started to present yourself toward me and of all the floors you decide to pick the sixth floor. Guess six is your lucky number."

"We do not like your trespassing, hunter." A disembodied voice said from the hallway.

"I heard that very clearly and I would like for you to speak to me again, so I can get a sense of your character and afterwards send you to the Other Side." Vail said.

"We demand you leave our home." The disembodied voice commanded.

"I'm not leaving this hotel until all of you are gone from it and it becomes nothing more than an old building waiting to be crumbled down."

A loud scream shrieked through the hallway, Vail covered his ears quickly to avoid minor damage to his ears. The shriek had immediately stopped. Vail removed his hands from his ears and the entire hallway was dead silent.

"Whatever you are and where ever you've come from, I am here to send you to another place where you will never escape your fate."

After searching the entire sixth floor, Vail continued to make his way upward toward the remaining floors, seven through thirteen. On the seventh floor, during Vail's searching of the rooms, he found a note which was left behind by someone who was either staying or working in the hotel. Vail read the note as it had implied there was some otherworldly force that dwelled before he hotel closed. Vail placed the note in his coat pocket.

"Seems you've been here a while." Vail said.

The eighth floor possessed neither anything related to the supernatural nor were any spirits contacted by Vail throughout the entire floor. The ninth floor possessed very little furniture and a shortage of rooms, whereas the first eight floors were settled with a total of twenty rooms where the ninth floor had a total of ten rooms. Vail kept his patience in check as he noticed there were no spirits being found within the upper floors.

"I know you're here and you are waiting on me to find you, yes?" Vail said. "I will find you and we will have our confrontation."

Vail stepped foot onto the tenth floor and spotted a difference in the air. A change of sorts which could only be caused by a weather effect, though it was continuing to snow on the outside, whereas the interior of the tenth floor felt a mixture of cold and heat. Vail had placed into his mind that he was dealing with a spirit or spirits that were unlike any he has encountered in his previous investigations.

"If you are on this floor with me, make yourselves known unto me." Vail said. "I heard one of you speak to me on the sixth floor and I demand that you speak to me now before I reach the thirteen floor and end this for good."

"Why have you come here, Travis Vail, the Spirit-Seeker." A voice said from the other end of the hallway. "You seem to be determined to eliminate us from our dwelling place and yet here we are."

Vail couldn't see the figure from the other end due to a dark mist covering its presence. Vail pulled out a flare and threw it toward the middle of the hallway. The flare lit up most of the hallway and all Vail could gather by his sight was a figure and on its hands were long sharpened nails and its eyes were like the cold sky to him.

"Come. Come Travis Vail. Follow me up to the thirteen floor and you will receive what you've come for." The voice said as it disappeared.

Vail ran toward the other end of the hall, fanning away the dark mist that covered the end. Vail saw nothing and ran up toward the thirteen-floor, surpassing the eleventh and twelfth floors. Vail ran unto he reached the door that would lead him to the thirteen-floor. Vail kicked the door opened and looked around, realizing that the floor was a place where people would stay. The thirteen-floor appeared to be an office of some kind, apparently a secret office.

"What kind of place is this?" Vail questioned.

"This is our dwelling place, Spirit-Seeker." The voice said. "As is mine."

The voice appeared closer toward Vail as the entity revealed itself to him. The entity appeared to be a hybrid of both man and demon. Vail took a step back as he stared at the creature, never seeing a living being of that kind before in his lifetime.

"What in the hell are you?"

"I am known throughout the ages as Kamagrauto, servant of Dagor, the Soul Eater."

"Dagor? Soul Eater? What in the hell are you speaking about, demon beast?!"

"It seems you've never studied in the occult as deep as you thought. We're always hearing about what your work has done for many in the world. From your little stop at a mansion to that forest of druids. We know of you, Spirit-Seeker."

Vail stared at Kamagrauto, scanning the room for any others that might appear before him on the thirteen floor.

"How have you been watching me? Why have you been watching me and for what purpose?"

"You are one of our enemies, Travis Vail."
Kamagrauto said. "You and countless others all share the same goal of eliminating our kind from this earth to leave only the righteous alive to subdue it."

"There aren't others like me, demon. If there were, I would've already made myself known to them."

"The intriguing part of this meeting here is all of you mostly have encountered one another in the past at some point in time. Whether it was a small crossover or a passing by on the road. You've all met at some point in time and you all will meet each other again in the coming future, but that will be the moment where all of you get agree to join sides to face us."

"This isn't making any sense. I'm about to send you over."

Vail pulled out his book and raised it over his head. Kamagrauto laughed at Vail for doing the task. He even started clapping his hands and rubbing his sharp nails together to sidetrack Vail's focus.

"That little book isn't going to work on me, Vail. I am beyond an ordinary spirit. I was created by my master Dagor and only through him may I be put away."

"I won't let you leave this place alive and intact, demon." Vail said. "You must leave this place and take the remaining spirits with you."

"Why do you think I'm here?" Kamagrauto said. "I'm here on orders from Dagor to collect as many souls as possible and bring them back to him for observation."

"What is he observing them for?"

"Why to consume them of course and go gain as much strength as he needs to succeed in his plans."

"I will not allow such destruction to be cause in my presence!" Vail said as he ran toward Kamagrauto.

"You small pest."

Kamagrauto lifted Vail up off the ground and threw him against the wall as a frame that was hanging on the wall fell onto his head, cutting his forehead open.

"Very well, I will be leaving now, Travis Vail and we will indeed come across paths once again. But, that day will most certainly be your final investigation."

Kamagrauto vanished in a puff of smoke as Vail ran after it. Seeing nothing but an empty room, Vail leaves the thirteen floor and travels back down to the first floor. The sun began to shine down on Vail as he walked outside and sealed the hotel doors shut. He entered his car and drove away. Though, in his mind was Kamagrauto's words of what would come concerning Dagor and others whose work was similar to Vail's own.

THE PARTY PEOPLE

A group of three men make their attempt to exchange deals with the other criminals within the city of Chicago. Making their move in the hours of the night to avoid civilian suspicion and possibly police eyes. The three men call themselves The Party People. Their names are Trystan, Charles, and Jordan. Known in Chicago as one of the top criminal gangs that can produce great deals. Be it drugs, weapons, or anything than the standard.

"You're sure you can get this done?" A thug asked.

"We've proven our track record." Trystan said. "Many times."

"So, we're all good?"

"We're good once you received what you've asked for. Until then, you're still on the watch list."

Exchanging the deals. The agreements are aligned as well is their partnership. Preparing to leave, they hear sudden footsteps coming toward them from the other direction. Near a corner. They stand guard, holding their firearms up toward the footsteps.

"Whomever is there, I suggest you take your next step and move it back to where you came."

From the corner appeared a man. Dressed in all black with a leather trench coat and sunglasses. His appearance and demeanor took the criminals off their guard. Unaware of such a figure walking around Chicago dressed like he was.

"Who the hell are you supposed to be?" Charles asked.

"I'm the man whom you'll all fear." The man declared. "From now on, I am the one who's about to put you into the ground."

"Into the ground how?" Jordan questioned.

"Very simple." The man said, raising up a pistol and firing it, hitting one of the men in the exchange.

"Shit!" Charles yelled. Seeing the man dead behind him and the blood flowing from his head.

"Who will be next to die?" The man asked. "I will be waiting patiently for the next fifteen seconds before making the decision myself."

"You won't kill any of us!" Trystan yelled.

"We'll see about that when the sun is up."

He fired his pistol once more, causing them to ruckus around the site. Running away as fast as possible while the man chased them down. Running behind them like a predator chasing his prey.

Trystan jumped into his truck as Charles and Jordan jumped in the back. Hasty to leave the area. Trystan started the engine before looking back through the mirror, seeing the man walking toward them.

"Guys." Trystan said, "He's coming."

Calm and still. Like he's not even in a hurry to kill them. His presence and walk set fear into their hearts.

"What are we going to do?" Jordan questioned in fear.

"We'll get back to the boss. Make our way to his location."

"I'm alright with that." Charles said. "Let's get out of here."

The truck started and drove off, leaving the man watching them leave the area. The truck made a quick turn and vanished from his sight. He nodded and smirked. Placing his pistol back into its holster. Settling his coat, he turned around and walked back to the site where the exchange was taking place.

"They had to leave something here for me to follow."

He searched the area and checked the pockets of the man he killed. Inside his jacket pocket, he found the man's cell phone. The man checked the phone and saw it was set on a map. The map featured a trail. The trail started in Chicago and made its way north into Canada. Into a city known for many crimes and strange occurrences.

"Retropolis."

He took the phone as he returned to his motorcycle. He checked the map once more, gathering a sure understanding. He nodded and rode off from the site as the police began to come to the scene.

<u>PREPARATION FOR THE COMING</u>

"I have returned to my home. My kingdom in this world. Only to discover there are those who dress themselves up as my allies, to only be enemies within our kindred clothing."

Rashad Tabari, the King of Mekeopia and known across the land of Africa as the Black Viscount returned to his kingdom after his training within the Order of Swords along with political deals regarding the peculiar mineral of the land referred to as quakerium. Those within Rashad's circle advised him not to share the mineral with those on the outside of the kingdom, yet, Rashad felt there were few outside of his rule that could strength the mineral's power for safety and protection causes. Mostly in the causes of measuring tremors and sudden earthquakes across the world. Kafar, one of Rashad's advisors dressed in a purple royal robe decorated with gold approached him as he entered the golden gates of Mekeopia.

"My lord. We have news to discuss with your future."

"What news, Kafar?"

"Madam Oyu has determined she will not tolerate you act of rule any longer. She requests an audience to cause war amongst you and her."

"Where did you hear this?"

"From the council. They believe your relations to the outsider may prove deadly to us rather than fruitful."

"Any others who agree with Oyu? Any from within our range?"

"The others you're familiar with. Air Shango and Kurto Hauko, the White Dagger."

Rashad nodded to his advisor's words. He turned to him with a smile as they entered the throne room of Mekeopia. Decorated in the features of the Black Viscount along with the crest of the Order of Swords above the throne seat. Kafar gestured his hand toward the Sword crest.

"They believe that to be the cause of our concern."

"The Order of Swords has done nothing but help us in our matters." Rashad said. "We have similar interests."

"Oyu and her followers believe in creating an Order of Swords within the Mekeopia range will only cause conflict with those within these lands, later, creating a war with those on the outside."

"Oyu hasn't met those I've encountered over my time. If she only had met them, maybe she would have a change in mindset."

"Maybe she would if you would speak to her."

"Speaking to her hasn't taken us anywhere, Kafar. It would only spark a fight within these walls. And we don't desire to have blood spilled upon the walls of the kingdom."

Rashad sat in the throne seat and Kafar stood before him. They continued their dialogue before Kafar had left the throne room. The doors had shut, leaving Rashad to mediate the news. He took a moment to pray toward the Sovereign of the Heavens. The deity who had awoke him after his father's death at the hands of Rage Killmaster. It was only after the moment where Rashad had met with the Order of Swords, who taught him the ways of their faith and their skills in war. Rashad had taken to heart their faith and their skills. He adopted their ways and returned home to make a change with himself and those in his land.

"Sovereign of the Heavens, I speak to you. I speak of your greatness. The things you're able to do, no one else can produce. Your power shows your might and your work shows its worth. I ask of you to lead me into making this decision. What must I do regarding my enemies. Should I take them into war or should I leave them to their own devices? I ask of it within your mighty power."

The following day, Madam Oyu had appeared at the gates of the kingdom. She stood there, decked out in her dress memorizing the ancient ways of the lost African cultures. She stood with her followers behind. Approaching her on both sides were Shango and Hauko. Shango carried a smoking skull in his hands and Hauko was decked out in a white uniform set with many daggers attached. From his chest to his waist to his ankles. Kafar ran to Rashad to tell him of the visitors. He stepped out and could see Oyu and her company standing. They stared him down.

"What shall we do?" Kafar asked.

Rashad looked out and seen the nearby homes were cleared out. The residents of the kingdom were no longer in the streets. Behind Rashad appeared the army of Mekeopia. Men and women prepared to fight. Rashad turned and stared at Oyu.

"Aren't you going to let us in, King Tabari?" Oyu gestured. "We only desire to speak."

"Why have you come with an army of your own and two bodyguards set out to do me harm?"

"Harm will only be done if it's necessary."

"And killing me is necessary of your cause of this visit?"

"To a degree. You knew better than to associate with those outsides of these lands. You broke every truce your ancestors placed upon this kingdom to suit your own will. Your own ideas will lead your people to an early grave."

"You believe so?"

"It is why I'm here. To overthrow you with the support of your people and to claim your family heirloom for myself. Mekeopia desires a change and it can only be accomplished by the hands of a woman. A strong woman."

Rashad turned toward Kafar, who is uncertain of his next moves.

"Grab my gear, quickly." Rashad whispered.

"Yes, my lord." Kafar replied, running into the palace.

"Give me a moment, Madam Oyu and the gates will be open."

They waited until Kafar came to Rashad with his suit. The suit of the Black Viscount. Rashad had entered his palace with the suit and as he entered the gates had open. Oyu was ecstatic. She raised up her arms toward the kingdom.

"Take Mekeopia!" She yelled to her army. "Take it for your pleasure and for your new coming queen."

The army ran into the kingdom and took the fight to Rashad's army. Inside the palace, Rashad started at the helmet of the Viscount suit. Within his being, he felt a presence. He closed his eyes and the answer he sought had come into him. It merged with his own being, taking over his mind and will. He opened his eyes and a smile had formed on his face.

The armies battled a bloody fight on the streets of

Mekeopia while Shango and Hauko awaited Rashad to exit his palace. They taunted him at every turn. During the fight, the palace doors had opened and walling out was Rashad, fully formed in the Black Viscount suit. The crown-formed cowl shook the presence of those on the streets. The black armor shined with the sun. The black cape had flowed with the wind and the sword gripped tightly his right hand.

"Who will be first." He asked.

Shango and Hauko ran toward the Black Viscount as the fight for Mekeopia had begun.

<u>RESTORING ONE'S MOTIVE</u>

Dameon Mason survived the battlefields of the Republic War. A war which resolved in undone circumstances. Throughout the war, many across the nations enlisted to fight for their country. Mason was recruited for the United States and fought alongside the partnering nations. In those battles, Mason met others such as himself on the field, including Commander Norland and his team of the Champions. The war was funded by many corporations in the service for weapons and vehicles.

"You're new to the force?" Norland asked.

"Somewhat." Mason answered. "What's with the chilly air out here?"

"It's a complicated issue with us on this side of the border." Norland laughed, rubbing his arms.

Hawke Industries was a primary seller in the war alongside KexInc. Cherub Enterprises was subtle in the war, but their presence was felt heavily when concerning themselves with techniques and stealth.

"I will give my services to the causes of the war." Nathan Hawke said in a press meeting. "You can trust me, and you can certainly trust my weapons."

"My designs will heavily change the face of the war." Kex Kendrick said. "From now on, you will be asking yourselves, "How could we win the war without the help of Kex Kendrick?"."

"Any word from those at Cherub?" A Lieutenant asked. "Anything from their leader?"

"Nothing." The General replied. "I don't think they're concerned with the war. Perhaps, they know more than we do of how to win this thing."

The armies continued to face each other whenever possible and no one ceased until there was victory.

"Run." Mason screamed on the field. "Run until you can get to the camp!"

Mason ran with his fellow soldiers on the field during a air strike by the opposing force. They were outnumbered and only seven of them remained. Mason did as much as he could in assisting his teammates. Many died from the impact of the air strikes and once Mason was near the safety area, his surrounds were bombed by the strikes. Mason was left unconscious and in serious pain. The medics arrived on the field, counting the dead and assisting the injured. None were as injured as Mason, who's arms were torn and legs from his knees to feet were heavily damaged. Even his torso was in dire need of emergency surgery.

During his surgery, the doctors knew Mason would die from his injuries. His arms and legs were amputated, and his chest was filled with shrapnel. They declared him dead. But before giving up on Mason, he was enlisted into a secret project. A test to see if the experiment could indeed work. Having been tested before and failing every time. Mason was now the next one in line for the test titled "Project: Bionics."

"He may not survive the surgery." A doctor said to the commanding officer.

"Just do the procedure." The officer said. "We'll deal about his survival afterwards. Whether he's alive or dead."

There, Mason was infused with bio-nanotechnology. His arms were replaced with bionic arms. His legs were replaced with knee to feet bionics. His chest was cleared of the shrapnel and in his chest, a reactor which held the power for Mason to move his new limbs. After the experiment, the doctors waited to see if Mason would survive the surgery and after two days, Mason awoke and gazed at his newly formed body.

"What's happened to me?"

"Mr. Mason, calm yourself." The doctor said. "Let us explain what's happened."

"What has happened to me?!"

His anger shouted as he fought off the doctors with

his bionic arms. Terrified at what's happened to him, Mason left the base after fighting off the doctors and the armored soldiers that were kept guarding the surgery room. Mason jumped, discovering his legs were detailed with hover packs. Giving him the ability to fly. Confused and enraged, Mason left and placed himself in an open field.

A dirty and beaten field. He gazed around, realizing he's landed in the same field where his injury began. He found what appeared to be an air strike missile on the ground. One that did not go off. Mason read the missile and what was labeled on it made him even more angry. He desired revenge. The biotech reactor in his chest glowed from its triangular corners. Mason felt the reactor in his chest and he could feel the flowing of blood moving through his arms and legs and through his chest. Learning what his body has become.

"What have I become. What have they done to me?"

Mason questioned his existence and he couldn't understand what really happened to himself after the incident. He could only feel anger inside and with that anger was vengeance. A thirst for it and Mason craved it. He wanted to return the favor to those on the opposing side as well as those involved with his newly bionic limbs and the reactor in his chest.

"Why." Mason questioned. "Of all people."

Mason yelled in a fit of rage and from his arms fired machine gun rounds. Mason stopped and glanced at his arms. The shine of them intrigued Mason to take closer looks. The arms stood out with the flowing glow of green moving through them. The similar color of the corners to the reactor. The color even flowed through the legs. Mason raised his left foot and beneath his feet, he found the boosters for his flight. Connecting from his ankles to his feet.

"What is all of this?"

Looking closer to his arms he found several rounds of ammunition in his arms. There was a muzzle place above his wrist and Mason stretched out his arms and with his mind was able to fire the rounds from his arm. Mason showed a faint smile, but still showing the signs of confusion and anger.

"The hell have they done to me?" Mason continued to question.

Mason took off into the air. Shaking and stumbling as he learned to control his flight. He knew he would have to cope with his new discovery and his goal was to find the ones responsible for his drastic change to his body and to his life. He could no longer live the life he had before the war. He is a soldier. A fallen soldier to many. The one thing on his mind was to confront to manufacturer of the missile which caused his life to change. The manufacturer's logo on the missile read– Hawke Industries.

KNOWING WHO YOU SERVE

"I had a life. It was taken from me without notice. Without hesitation. That day, I learned there was another side to everything and it was at that moment, I became who I am this day."

A figure cloaked in a dark blue cape. The cape extended far beyond average length to the human body. His body was covered in black and gold armor. Rough in detail and somewhat scaly to touch. The figure reached the top of a church and stood still. His eyes glowing as fine gold. A mouth could not be seen nor could ears and a nose. He watched the streets of the city move with cars. He could spot civilians walking along the sidewalks.

"This world, it isn't all its talked up to be. I learned that day this world is temporary. People build up treasures on this earth, only to leave them behind after they're dead. Their treasures and possessions crumble underneath the weight of the dust and the homes of the moths."

The figure kept his gaze upon the city and its people. He remained there for hours on end. It wasn't until near daybreak where he was visited by an angel. The angel's name is Ananchel. The figure arose from his stance, almost as if he was a living statue atop the church as of the gargoyles.

"Creed." Ananchel said. "I need your help."

"My help? What for and what of?"

"Adrambadon is coming to this world in full force. He has an army behind him. Ready to take the orders he spews out."

"Do you know who may be in this army of his?"

"I saw those of The Cult. The hooded ones. I even glimpsed the demon Abacus, the beast known as Satanic, and I saw legions of tormented souls marching behind them. They're ready for a war on this earth."

"And you desire to have me find him and his army before things get out of hand?"

'As always. You're a different breed of character, Creed."

"I am no different than those who have come before me in this similar state. Humans can assist your causes better than I can."

"They don't have your strength. Your speed. Your reflexes. Even, your knowledge of the supernatural realms."

"Are you sure of that?"

"Very sure. Which is why I've come to you. Trust me, there are others who can help in this cause. But, they're busy with missions of their own. All of us are in this day and hour."

Creed removed himself from the top of the church, standing beside its giant cross. He thought to himself of Ananchel's motives and the words she spoke. It wasn't clear to Creed if he should take up the cause, yet, he could sense he was meant to prepare for something.

"If I take up arms in this fight, I don't do it for you and I don't do it for this Madam who's been discussed by many."

"Then, you will you do it for?"

"The one who saved me from working alongside Adrambadon in the beginning."

"Ah." Ananchel nodded. "I see."

Creed walked over to the edge of the church, gazing down at the open road. The sun began to pour out from the clouds above him. He began to absorb the sun's rays. Ananchel could only watch the scenery.

"When will you start with us?" She wondered.

"You'll find me when you'll see." Creed declared. "Remember, I am not far away. As you have managed to find me this day."

Creed jumped from the church and in the air, he flew. His cape spread across the sky to where those on the ground could see him. The span of the flowing, shining cape was tremendous and it would confuse the people to a small plane moving through the sky. Ananchel flew off and Creed vanished like a shadow into the morning sky.

A CON MAN'S GAME

"Hey, man. It's my call."

The man slammed a card onto the table. An ace card. Sitting within a bar. A bar filled with folkloric creatures and those of various mythologies. From fairy to beast. The man sitting at the table playing a game of cards with an orc. A brutish one, smelly, and covered in what may be its own sweat or the fluids of someone else's. the orc held up a card of his own. An ace. Pressing it against the table top.

"Looks like you've lost this round, boy." The orc said with a grim smirk.

"Have I now?" The man said. "Seriously?"

He held up another card. A king. The orc locked his eyes toward the card as the man sat it to the table. Beside the ace. The man smiled while the orc groaned in annoyance.

"Looks like YOU'VE lost this round." The man said laughing. "Boy!"

The orc slammed his fist against the table. Angry at the loss of the game. While the man prepared himself to leave the bar, getting up from his seat, the orc spotted something strange happening atop the table. The king card glowed and reverted into clubs. The orc noticed and stared at the man, who also saw the reverted card.

"Sorry about that." The man said, holding his hands up with a grin.

"You cheated!" The orc yelled. "You cheated!"

"Hey, just relax and we'll play again." The man bargained. "That is if you're willing to lose another round."

The orc bolted himself from the chair as the man ran out of the bar. The orc chased him and eventually lost him within seconds. The orc turned to every corner near the bar entrance looking for the man. On both sides, he cannot find any trace of him.

"Bastard!" The orc said before returning into the bar.

Down the streets, coming from around another block is the man himself. Smiling and grinning at his game win. Fixing his light-brown duster and his cargo, baggy-like clothing before walking away. He brushed his dirty blonde hair from his face before taking another step.

"Every time." He said, flipping a gold coin. A coin that belonged to a leprechaun.

While walking, he started to sense something around him. Preferably behind him. He continued walking and the sense intensified after each step he took. He decided to a stop and nodded. Letting out a low sigh. He knew something was about to happen.

"Alright, who's following me?" He said, turning around to see the orc from the bar, accompanied with three of his fellow friends. Another orc, a goblin, and a satyr.

"You didn't think I could just let that game slide by now." The orc said.

"We have a problem here." The man pointed.

"Yes, we do."

"No." The man mentioned. "I don't mean the card game. I mean the fact that you and your three ugly friends are out in the streets of Manchester in the daytime. Out in the open."

"What's it to you?" The goblin snarled.

"Aren't you afraid of humans seeing your faces?"

"The humans aren't our concern." The orc said. "Just you are."

The man nodded. Pointing toward them. Knowing what is about to take place and he's somewhat excited about it.

"You plan to kill me don't you?" He asked with a smirk.

"Damn right!" The orc yelled. "You cheated the game and you defiled our place of community."

"Defiled it? How?"

"By showing up without an invitation." The satyr said. "No one ever invited you to our place."

"True. But, I thought I would just come and go on my own terms. I mean, I've done it before in many other places. Thought, it would be the same. Somewhat."

"This isn't a human's game!"

"No. It is not. But, I'm playing anyway."

The man set his eyes on the four. Marking their place of stance as they moved around him. Measuring him for an attack. He relished in their movements. Preparing himself for something they don't see coming.

"Who wants to start this game of our first?" The man asked.

The cloudy day immediately turns into a rainy one. The man grins, staring at the four.

"Come on. Who's first."

The other orc ran for the man, yet, he was prepared and fired a ball of energy from his hands. Tossing the orc in the distance. Startling the others. The man smirked toward them with a hint of a wink.

"I don't have all day now."

The goblin went in for an attack. The man moved and snatched the goblin by one of his ears, quickly whispered something into it. The goblin fell back and stared at the man. His eyes gleam toward him. Seeing something he hasn't seen in ages. The goblin stood to his feet and in haste runs off. The satyr saw what happened to the goblin and turned to the man.

"You want to be next or something, goat-man?" The man said.

The satyr ran off himself. The orc watched him running. Confused to the whole reason as to why he chose to run away.

"Where in the hell are you going?!" The orc yelled. "Ekrac!"

"Looks like Ekrac will be taking some time to compose himself." The man gestured. "I recommend a few days tops. Maybe a week if he can handle the presences."

"What did you do to him?"

"I whispered a little spell I'm familiar with." The man said. "One that brings back those of the dead to haunt the living. Whichever hear the spell cast preferably."

"I've never dealt with a human of your kind before."

"So, I've heard from your kind. You folktale, fairy tale beings. Strange to know a human is aware of your world and is living amongst you. Far different than the average humans in the world today. Unlike them, I know of your world's existence and I happily volunteer in it. For the right price of course."

"You won't get away with cheating me."

"Oh. I think I will get away with more than that."

The man flared a flash of light in the face of the orc. Temporarily blinding him as the man smoothly robbed him of the money pouch attached to his belt.

"What did you do to me?!" The orc asked, holding his eyes.

"I shut your eyes for a moment." The man said.

"Don't worry. You'll be seeing things again very soon. As if this whole scenario never took place."

The man walked away from the area while the orc attempted to search for him with his hands. Waving his arms around. Trying to grab the man before he left. The orc could only hear the footsteps of the man as they dissipated from the location.

"You're a con artist!" The orc yelled in anger.

"You're absolutely right!" The man said. "Thinking you were playing your own game, you were playing mine. It's a con man's game in this world."

"I will find you and I will make you pay for this. For all of this!"

"I hope so." The man said, turning around to face him with a smile. "Look for the man they call Fable. You'll find me."

The orc remembered that day and has never forgotten—The Man Called Fable.

EPOCH ONE

I

Professor Cullen Edge had a vision. A vision of the world where humanity and nubreeds could live together in peace. It was the beginning of his life's purpose. Edge decided to find a location outside of Chicago, Illinois. He did and discovered a large home. Preferably a mansion-sized home. Edge bought the home and proclaimed it to be the beginning of his vision's work.

Edge traveled across the world to find the nubreeds worthy of his vision. Traveling to the city of Salt Lake City, entering a bar. Edge searched out the bar and found a man playing pool. The man was young and lean. His short long black hair covered a portion of his face. He was fair to look upon by the opposite sex. His face slightly aged, but inexperienced. Edge approached the man as he caught his attention.

"Sorry, sir." The young man said. "You'll have to pay

to play me."

"I haven't come to play a game of pool, young man."

"Then why are you standing here. In front of the table?'

"I've come to have a word with you."

"With me? What for?"

"I know what you are."

The young man's eyes moved slowly toward Edge. Edge gave the man a nod of secrecy and he nodded back. Moving closer toward him.

"What do you want with me?"

"To join the cause."

"Cause?"

"Yes. A cause that will shape this world for the better. Where you no longer have to hide what you are from humanity."

"What makes you so sure?"

"Because I am one such as yourself. Abilities differ of course."

"You know what I can do?"

"I can sense your energy. What you can do appears in the currents of the air."

"Anyone else joined your little crusade?"

"I haven't spoken to another." Edge clarified. "You're the first on the list."

"The first?" The man gestured. "Well, that's… a first."

"What's your name?" Edge asked.

"Marth Randolph, Jr. Friends in the inner circle call me Valinor."

"Interesting. You already have a name hidden in the under layers."

"I didn't' choose it. My abilities apparently resembled something to the name. others like myself gave it to me. Called it a gift."

"It is a gift."

Edge looked around the bar. Seeing nothing but older men drinking and younger women watching the young men do their best to impress them. Marth continued playing pool. Nearly finished with his solo game.

"Are you doing anything in the next few days?"

"Nothing but moving on about across the country. A road trip I gave myself."

"Occupation?"

"Freelancer of many things. It keeps me on a clear schedule."

"How about joining me. I'm sure you can clear your schedule for just a few days."

Marth hit another ball into the hole. He stood and looked at Edge. He thought in his mind.

"Am I the only one you're looking for?"

"No. There are others I have to pay visits."

"Any possibility of a fight ahead?"

"I would never say never."

Marth nodded with a grin and placed the pool stick onto the table. He took one last drink of his beer and grabbed his leather jacket. Putting it on.

"After you, sir." Marth said.

Marth left with Edge on his journey.

Their next location of travel was Italy. Making their entrance into Venice, Edge walked, and Marth followed. Marth took looks at the Italian women he saw passing him and Edge.

"I have to guess who's here you're looking for?"

"You'll see her once we find her."

"Any idea where this woman might be?" Marth asked with a nod. "Does she look like any of them we've passed by so far?"

"I can't say. Maybe. Maybe not."

"It would be helpful."

"You can decide that when we meet her."

"Have you spoken to her at least? Unlike making the same appearance you did to me?"

"Actually, I have. She was inclined to learn more about my vision of the future and she agreed to join immediately."

"Did she?"

"Yeah."

"She sounds young."

"By joining in haste?"

"Yeah. A little too young for my taste."

"Don't get caught in the affection of many before

you. Some may entrap you."

"You sound like the older heads who came before me."

"They had a point in terms of affections."

They continued to walk, and they came across a diner. Entering the diner, Edge searched the place as he did with the bar and he saw a young woman standing behind the counter. Marth looked around and couldn't imagine which woman is the one Edge is looking for.

"You see her yet?" Marth asked.

"I'm already ahead of the clock."

Edge approached the counter, inching closer toward the young woman with the red hair and brown eyes. You could tell she was a native of Italy. Once the woman caught a glimpse of Edge standing at the counter, she jumped up. She screamed, gaining the focus of all in the diner. Marth held his head down, looking out of the windows. The woman calmed down and Edge greeted her with a smile. She was happy to see him.

"Good to finally meet you, Ariana."

"You came." She said. "You actually came."

"I did, and you know why."

"I do. So, it's time I guess."

"It is."

Ariana grabbed whatever belonged to her and told the owner of the diner she was leaving for the college internship. Ariana left with Edge and Marth. She glanced over at Marth, looking at his features. She leaned in toward Edge.

"Is he part of your vision too?"

"He is. Don't get any ideas. Please."

"No worries. I was just curious."

They left Italy on Edge's private plane. Within the plane, Marth sat in front of Edge and witnessed how excited Ariana was to have finally met him.

"You dreamed of this moment?" Marth asked her.

"I have. Ever since he contacted me about forming his team. I couldn't turn such an offer down."

"You never said what this group is supposed to do besides help the world."

"When I have all of you assembled, I will let you know the true intent of this collaboration." Edge declared. "Believe me, the world will be better of it."

"You must have some codename." Marth said toward Ariana.

"Codename?"

"You know. One that only those like yourself will call you."

"Oh. Like a secret name."

"Yeah. You have one?"

"Friends call me Gale."

"Gale?" Marth looked over to Edge with confusion. "I'm not understanding why they chose that for a name?"

"She can control the elements of the wind, Marth. Her emotions will determine their full strength She can emit pleasant winds, or she can conjure winds up to the strength of hurricanes and tornadoes."

"Intriguing." Marth said, sitting back in his seat. "I'll make sure not to get on your bad side."

"No need to concern yourself, Mr.?"

"Just call me Marth."

"I was going to ask of your codename."

"Oh." Marth smirked. "Valinor."

"I like it."

"Great." Marth shook his head slightly.

"So, what can you do?"

"Different things. Manipulate matter to my own use. Create energy beams in the form of lightning or transfer them into object. Somewhat of a kinetic-type of energy."

"That sounds pleasant."

"Not when someone pisses me off." Marth detailed. "Professor Edge, where are we going next?"

"We're going to meet another woman who's keen on helping this cause."

"Keen huh?"

"Yes. Unlike he both of you, she's somewhat already involved in the helping process. Just on her own terms for now."

"Where is she now?" Ariana wondered.

"Back in the States. Somewhere moving around Michigan."

"Should be easy to find her." Marth said. "She's probably doing things in Detroit."

"How can you be sure of that?"

"Detroit seems lie the kind of place you'll find those like us. Nubreeds."

"I'll take your word for it." Edge said, contacting the pilot.

The plane made its travel toward Detroit. Upon landing, they learn the city is being protected by a blonde-haired Caucasian woman dressed in a white and blue uniform. Reports had claimed she was able to create ice and snow from her hands, using the element as a tool against criminals. Hearing the news, Edge smiled with relief. Ariana only wondered, and Marth didn't understand.

"Must be her." Marth said. "I'm guessing. Unless, you're looking for someone who can conjure fire?"

"No. She's the one." Edge said. "They call her Lois Frost."

"Seriously." Marth looked. "What a name."

They roamed the streets of Detroit and within an instant, they see several criminals attempting to rob a jewelry store. Marth and Ariana want to help stop them, but Edge held them back.

"Let her come." Edge said.

Around the corner, a large flow of ice came in, ramming the criminals from the store. Atop the ice stood Frost. Glowing and emitting small embers of ice. She stopped the criminals by freezing their legs to the pavement. after stopping them, she turned around to see Edge.

"Professor?" She said, approaching him.

"You knew I would come."

"I've been waiting." She hugged Edge tightly. Glancing over to Marth and Ariana. "Who are they?"

"Members of what we have coming."

"So, it's happening now?"

"Afraid so. You're not busy, are you?"

"Actually, my schedule just cleared up."

"Then come with us. We have four more to recruit before we can officially start."

"Four?" Marth asked. "Four more?"

"Yes. We need a team. Only a team can do what I've already spoken."

Frost walked with them on their way to the plane in a new change of casual clothes apart from her other uniform. Edge gave her the information needed to bring her up to speed. She took in everything as if it was water soaking into her being.

"Where's the next location, Professor?"

"There's a young man in Miami. His skills will prove useful in this."

"Don't say he's a swimmer." Marth said.

"What do you think? A young man living on the beach."

"Should've kept my mouth shut."

"It happens." Edge said humorously.

Down in Miami, Edge and his group walked along the coast. looking at the beach. The sand covered with tourists soaking themselves in the sun. children run through the area. They saw a few young men surfing the waters. Marth stared at them.

"You see him?"

"Not now."

"What does he look like?" Lois asked. "Would be easier to spot him if we all knew his features."

"Just watch the water."

"Why?" Marth asked.

"He'll show himself." Edge declared. "His boastfulness cannot be held down by anyone. Even those who fear those like himself."

As they watched, a sprout of water busted from the beach. The people scattered closer to see the sprout and standing atop the sprout was a young man with brown hair and blue eyes. He cheered on the beach as the sprout held its balance. Marth saw it and turned to Edge, who nodded.

"He controls water. Great."

"That's him." Edge said.

"He has no shame in keeping it to himself." Marth said.

"We have to get him." Lois said. "Keep this all quiet before the authorities get here."

"How come they didn't stop you in Detroit?" Ariana asked.

"Because they were afraid of me. Afraid of trying to stop me from doing good. That's why I was spared trouble."

They moved quickly to get near the water. Almost stepping into the shore, Edge shouted out to get the young man's attention. He saw Edge standing at the shore with Marth, Ariana, and Lois. He recognized them and their appearance. It differed from the rest of the public. He transformed the sprout into a wave and surfed his way back to shore, where he stopped in front of Edge. The public could only watch.

"I recognized you guys. You're different than the rest."

"You know why we're here?" Edge said. "We need you to come with us."

"No way. I'm not going to jail for having a little bit of fun."

"I'm not talking about jail."

"So, what are you talking about?"

"Doing the world a bit of good for once. Give you the chance to use your gift to suit a higher purpose rather than having vanities of fun."

"I see. What do I get paid?"

"Excuse you." Lois said, stepping up to him. "Who said you deserve any kind of payment?"

"Did I offend you, ma'am?"

"You want to find out?"

"Don't make me throw you into the water."

"I'll freeze the water before you make a move."

"For real?!" He asked with excitement. "Show me!"

"Lois, step back." Edge said. Lois took a step back. "It would be best if you could come with us. Whatever you might achieve is up to you. But, the bigger picture is helping those like yourself living in this world with peace."

"Wait. You're all nubreeds?"

"Yes. We are." Marth said. "Are you coming with us or what?"

He thought and in his mind, was the possibilities of traveling the world. He couldn't turn down an offer like it. He nodded quickly and shook Edge's hand.

"I'm in."

"Just like that?" Lois asked.

"Yeah. Figured I could have fun doing a bit of good."

"Quite." Marth said.

"Very well." Edge said. "Let's leave and gather the other three."

The young man changed his clothes and left with them to the plane. While entering the plane, they asked for his name. his name is Daniel Summers and those in his inner circle have given him the name of The Surf. Marth turned his head away after hearing it being said.

"This is a joke."

"What?"

"They call you The Surf?"

"Yeah. Sounds cool."

"To you. To me, it sounds like a drink or a campy fellow in a costume."

"Works too."

Edge made their next travel to find another young woman. One who possesses the ability to wield magic to her use. Making their way into another state, Nevada. They arrived in Las Vegas. During the night, they made plans to find her and to leave as quickly as they could. Fearing they would be confronted by Vegas' own hero who patrols the city during the night.

"She is within one of the casinos." Edge said.

"How do you know?" Marth asked. "She is gambling or something related?"

"She works here. Standard part-time job."

"You really have all of us down." Lois mentioned.

"It's part of the planning process, Lois. You know how it all works out."

"That I do."

Walking within one of the casinos, they hear cheering coming from down the other area. They made a move toward the spot and there they saw her. Dancing for the crowd. Her black hair wowed the audience. Her emerald eyes increased the number of viewers, and her countenance was more beautiful than most of the women within the casino. The crowd loved her moves.

Her belly dancing stole the show according to the audience. Marth found her attractive and he kept it to himself. Lois wasn't sure she is the one Edge had come for.

"Are we in the right place?"

"Yes. We are." Edge said. "Just need to find a way to get her over here."

"The crowd looks like they're in a trance." Marth mentioned.

"They are." Edge replied. "Part of her traits."

"Just call her out." Daniel said. "Shouldn't be a problem."

"We don't need you to do that."

"Relax, cold woman."

"Don't call me that."

"Just. Chill." Daniel smiled. "I know you can do that."

"This little runt."

"Lois, settle yourself. No need to attack your teammates ahead of schedule."

After she finished her dancing, she walked down to the floor and Edge stood before her. She looked around as the rest of the team approached her. Fear had gripped her.

"Is there an issue?" She asked.

"No that concerns you, honey." Daniel muttered.

"Ignore him." Lois said, pushing Daniel back from her.

"I am Professor Cullen Edge, and this is my team. We've come to recruit you."

"Recruit me? What for?"

"I know you're a nubreed and I know what you can do."

"I don't understand what you're talking about."

"You had those people under a trance." Marth said. "Come on, just hear him out."

She took a moment and listened to Edge. He told her about his vision and how he's aware of those such as her. She listened as the rest of the team waited outside. Marth checked his watch occasionally. Daniel stared at the women walking around the casino. Ariana and Lois talked about traveling the world. Marth glanced up, seeing Edge and the young woman walking toward them.

"She's agreed to join us." Edge said.

"Good to hear." Lois said. "What's your name?"

"Isabel Dotson."

"What do others call you?"

"Magic Carpet."

"Really?" Daniel asked. "Why?"

"My coat." She showed her coat. Layered in many colors. Mainly gold, violet, and emerald. "My coat was made from the elements of a magic carpet."

"Impressive." Ariana said.

"Indeed." Lois replied.

They left Vegas and made their final travel to a private school in Sacramento, California. Entering the city. Edge moved swiftly to gain the final two members for his team. Picking the right hour and day to make his visitation to them. Nearing the school, Edge spotted the two young men standing outside talking with each other. He exited the car and approached them. They turned and could only wonder.

"Don't fear me." Edge said. "I've come to speak with the two of you for something special."

"Like what?"

"Do you desire to help the world and grant a life of peace to those like yourselves?"

They stared and looked at each other before facing Edge. They saw he others standing behind at the car.

"You're all nubreeds too?"

"We are."

Edge spoke with them and afterwards, he brought them along. Returning to the plane, Edge looked, and he had his team assembled. They only needed a name. while the plane was in the air making its return to the homestead, Edge meditated as the team talked and learned about each other. The two men were Scott Branagh and Danny Blake, known to themselves and the group as Emerald and Hailstone. Emerald could project energy beams from his eyes in the color of green and Hailstone was able to conjure and create particles of ice.

Similar to Lois, yet his power could be conjured within heated areas.

Somewhere else, Raymus Eisenhower, a close friend of Edge's stood in an undisclosed location in front of seven other nubreeds. Their appearances ranged from tall to terrifying to intimidating. Raymus gave them a speech and promised them the world would fully be in the hands of the nubreed under his fellowship. A fellowship of nubreeds.

II

Edge and his team returned to the homestead in Chicago. There, the team walked through the home and picked out the rooms where they'll be staying for the foreseeable future. Edge went into his office and discovered on the news, there was an ongoing attack downtown. The others ran into the office, seeing the footage. Downtown, Raymus' fellowship had begun attacking humans. Raymus saw the news crew and demanded them to turn the camera toward him. Raymus stared into the camera. Fully clad in his orange and black uniform with his metallic helmet only revealing his eyes as the rest of his face was hidden in the thick shadow.

"To all nubreeds witnessing this event, I ask of you to join me. Join us in the fellowship. Here, you can no longer deal with being feared, ridiculed, or hated by humanity. Here, you can be loved, cherished, and at peace."

Edge turned off the TV as his group waited for some response. He turned toward them, and Daniel waved his hands.

"I think we should help those people."

"Really?" Lois asked. "I mean, how are we supposed to fight other nubreeds?"

"Simple." Marth said. "We face them together."

"Didn't we just get here?" Daniel mentioned. "I mean, I just picked out my room and now you're saying we're about to go into the city to fight other nubreeds?"

"It seems to be the case." Edge replied. "It is what I've brought you all together for. To protect humanity and to gain peace by doing so."

"Then, let's go." Marth said with a grin.

The team headed out to downtown where they met Raymus and his fellowship. The members of the fellowship were called Cosmic Card, a man who could control kinetic energy like Marth. Mistress Destroyer, a woman who possessed sharp metallic claws within her fingers that reached long lengths. Omega Thunder, a brute of a man who wielded titanium whips that emitted electricity. X-Manta, an undersea hunter who can breathe underwater and live above the ground. He has a background in the skills of being a mercenary. The Marine, a fellow nubreed who once was a member of the military in secrecy and participated in several of their secret projects to create super soldiers. Eerie, a woman whose outward appearance matched her ability to possess magic at a great scale. She also delves deeper into the dark magic of the universe. and Jackhammer, a man whose body is used as a demolition tool.

"Who are these guys?" Daniel asked.

"Raymus levitated himself toward them. Standing between his and Edge's teams. Raymus nodded at Edge. Showing a hint of respect.

"Why have you come? Truthfully."

"We've come to put a stop to your terrorizing activities." Edge said. "Why else would we be here?"

"You don't desire to join the fellowship?"

"We do not. It's not the right way, Raymus."

"And how would you understand?"

"You know me very well. You understand where I'm coming from with my words."

Raymus was disgusted with Edge' words and moved back with his team. The teams were prepared to fight against each other. The civilians of Chicago came out and watched the team stare down. They recorded the event with their phones and the nubreeds noticed quickly. Raymus wasn't pleased with the crowds of humans coming close.

"This isn't working properly." Raymus said. "I'm sorry to inform you, Edge, we must do this another time. My team hasn't properly gained their skills in dealing with their kind on the opposing side."

"Opposing? We're trying to develop a peace between nubreeds and humans."

"And that is where you're wrong. It will go wrong as it has before and then, you'll learn from your humanistic mistakes."

"It's called hope, Raymus."

"You're delusional, old friend. Very much like those who came before us. You'll fall into the same fate, I'm afraid."

Raymus turned to his team and signaled their leave. They left downtown with the humans surrounding Edge and his team. They were curious of their presence and somewhat scared.

"What do we do now?" Marth asked.

"We return to the homestead. Discuss further things there."

Making their leave and returning home, the footage of their confrontation with Raymus' fellowship spread across the internet. Edge wasn't pleased to an extent as some of the team members were excited. Proclaiming themselves to having become famous. Marth and Lois entered Edge's office, seeing him watching clips of the footage.

"We aren't disturbing you, Professor?" Lois asked humbly.

"No. Please, come in."

Marth and Lois sat in front of Edge. He turned off the computer and faced them. Shaking his head.

"I don't know what we'll do about Raymus and his group."

"They seem determined." Marth said. "As if they already have the answers to the cause."

"Raymus and I share a different view of the world and it's always been that way."

"You know each other I could tell."

"We grew up almost as brothers. But, our differences in views and opinions about the world caused a rift between us. Nearly torn for good. I've tried to make reason with him almost at every moment, yet. He appears to have been consumed with his methods. He wants humans extinct and he has recruited a team to do the job."

"We'll be there to stop them." Lois said. "At any cost."

"I agree with her." Marth smiled.

Edge nodded with a smile of his own. He stood up from the desk and looked. He thought.

"You guys need a team name."

"What did you have in mind?" Lois asked.

"There was a name that I came across when I was younger. Me and Raymus would call ourselves after that name."

"Do you remember it?" Marth asked.

"I do." Edge walked over to the bookshelf and

grabbed and old book. He opened it and inside was the name.

"We called ourselves the *Yonderers*."

<u>WE ARE WHO WE ARE</u>

"We left our home. A home far away from our sights now and we haven't even looked back. Not once."

A massive spacecraft hovered above a planet. Making itself an entrance around the planet's northern region. The ship, hovering with no sound emitting from the structure, lowered down into the planet's atmosphere. Sinking slowly as if the planet was quicksand.

"Yet, after leaving our home. A beacon discovered this planet. Its inhabitants walk upright, just as we do, and they have their own governments and civilizations. Just as we do."

The ship entered the atmosphere and landed near a set of mountains. Covered in ice and snow. The ship settled on the ground, cracking the rocks beneath it. The door opened upon the ship and its inhabitants exited. Walking in order with militaristic behavior. They appeared human, yet they were not. The final two to exit the ship appeared to look like a man and woman, yet they were taller than the average human.

"What are we to do here, Halo?" The woman asked.

"We make a living on this planet." Halo said. "This can be our new home."

Another one of the inhabitants approached Halo. Gazing around the snowed in mountains around them and looking toward the sky, seeing the clouds and the clear blue hidden.

"What is the name of this planet again, boss?"

"The inhabitants here call it Earth."

The space beings stare out and what they see is a valley, a valley of mountains, rivers, and snow. It impressed them greatly. Never have they seen such features on a planet before. Halo, the leader of the group turned to the woman figure.

"Aquila." Halo said. "We need to make sure the others are aware of this planet."

"There's no reason to invite them here. Imagine what they'll end up doing to the planet and its inhabitants."

"I understand your concern."

"Then, you are aware they cannot know we're here. They can't, Halo."

Halo nodded with a slight sigh of an exhale. He turned to Aquila, his wife. Holding her. Aquila's red hair flowed with the cold breeze of the mountains and their armor gleamed from the sunlight.

"Do not worry yourself over them. Romanus isn't

here. Therefore, there is no trouble."

Aquila nodded. "But, what if he learns of our presence here. He will come, and he will attempt to kill not just us, but the inhabitants of this planet."

Individually, they are named Halo, Aquila, Cygnus, and Ophiuchus. The group called the Royal Elite. They were the symbol of royalty back on their homeland, before being driven off by Romanus Dakingor. Regarded as the megalomaniac who desires complete control over the Elite and all species in the universe.

The Elite traveled across the valley in the ship, searching for the inhabitants of the planet. They came across a small town. Looking at the small buildings and homes.

"They have structures like ours." Aquila said. "But, they are far less advanced than what we once possessed."

"You are right about it, Aquila." Halo said. "They have strength, just as we do."

Cygnus, another member of the Elite approaches Halo and Aquila, pointed toward the ground, seeing one of the inhabitants working in a field. They spotted him, questioning the motives.

"What do you suggest we do?" Halo asked.

"I figure we can speak to it." Cygnus said. "See what they know and learn from them. That way we can fit in amongst them and never be set-apart."

"They do have an appearance like ours, but their feeble compared to us."

"What if it runs away?" Aquila asked. "What if our presence frightens it?"

"That will be understandable."

"Why?"

"Because we were feared on our world. Would make sense if it would flow here. Our aura has that ability."

Halo proceeded to land the craft upon the field. On the ground, the man is a farmer. He looked up, seeing the ship landing on the field. He took several steps back as the ships settled. The wind blew around him, holding his hat on his head. The wind calmed and from the ship exited the Elite. They approached the farmer and he stared at them. Questioning in his mind who they are and what they may want.

"Who are you people?" The farmer asked.

Halo turned to Aquila and she looked at the farmer. They listened to his speech and through it managed to reverse their own vocal cords and Aquila spoke to the farmer in his own language.

"We have come to your planet to learn about it and its inhabitants. Such as yourself."

"Is that right?" The farmer said. "Well, hate to bring it to you, but, you're not the first ones to come here."

"What do you mean?" Halo asked quickly.

"There have been others."

"What kind of others?"

"Others with abilities and features such like yourselves."

Aquila trembled slowly, believing Romanus had already arrived with his army. Halo glared toward her, calming her.

"Can you show us what they look like?" Halo asked.

"As a matter of fact, I can. Come with me."

They followed the farmer back to his home, which sat in the outskirts of the small town. Within the home, the Elite noticed picture frames, plants, and furniture.

"This looks like home." Aquila said.

"How can you show us how they looked?"

"Give me a moment, sir." The farmer said, grabbing a newspaper from the nearby drawer. Holding the paper, he approached the Elite and handed them the paper.

"See for yourselves."

Halo opened the paper and saw the main article. Titled, "*Nubreeds Among Us.*" The paper featured a photo of the group of young individuals rallied together with the term written beneath it.

"They call themselves the Yonderers?" The farmer said.

"Do you know where they're from?" Aquila asked.

"Absolutely. They're from here. Born and raised on this planet."

"Then, how come you're not one of them?"

"I wasn't born with their genes."

"It's a genetic makeup." Halo said. That's what this paper is telling us?"

"Yes. They were born with those powers of theirs and

there's more of them being born every year now."

"When did this all begin?"

"About three years ago to be precise. Along with all the others strange appearances."

"There are others?" Halo asked.

"Many of them."

Halo handed the farmer the paper, turning to the Elite.

"It appears this planet will be our new home. We need to contact and meet these "nubreeds." They may know something we don't."

"Maybe they can help us understand what's been happening."

"Perhaps so. Thank you for aiding us."

"It was my pleasure." The farmer said.

"We don't fear you?" Aquila asked.

"No. You do not. I've seen enough things in the past three years to where I'm used to circumstances like this."

Halo nodded as they prepare to leave the home.

"I have to ask." The farmer said. Getting Halo's attention. "What are you and where are you from?"

"We from a planet far from here." Halo said. "Those of other worlds have deemed us the Unkinds."

"The Unkinds?" The farmer questioned strangely.

"We are who we are." Halo declared.

The Elite left the home, returning to their ship. The farmer walked out, witnessing the ship hover and vanish like a bolt of lightning through the sky. The farmer shook his head with a smirk.

"Gets me every time."

TARGETED

1875. An old town in the Northern West of Canada. Four men dressed in dirty suits and hats exit out of a nearby saloon. They laugh and yell at each other. Enjoying the company. Each of the hats were a different color to differentiate the four men from those outsides of their circle. From the looks of them, they maintained control over the entire town. From the sheriff's department to the poorest one in the town. Their hats were gray, brown, white, and black.

"We've done everything we could've possibly achieved." The Black Hat said.

"In this town we have." The White Hat responded. "Yet, we haven't found him yet."

"I'm sure he'll come across our path sooner than later." The Brown Hat said. "He has to. You know the mindset of a man like him. Full of anger and yet, no direction."

"You really believe what you've spewed from your

mouth?"

"What else can you describe such a man like him?"

"Men like him make no mistakes. Their mind is always set on the mission. Until the mission is fulfilled, they're never satisfied. Never."

"He'll show himself." The Gray Hat said with vigor. "Trust my words, boys."

From their left, they could hear footsteps. Boots touching the ground with a clicking sound following the steps. Coming across them in the distance is a brown horse with its rider. The horse ran toward the four hats and stopped within only a few feet from their faces. The four hats were concerned and unaware as to who's riding the horse. Truthfully, the only thing that peaked their interests was the horse and the potential to have the rider join their circle.

The rider removed himself from the horse, dressed in all brown clothing with a black duster and hat. His face was hidden by the brim of the hat and his hands were set on his sides. He started to walk toward the four hats and they still weren't sure of what to make of the whole scene. The man in the brown hat stepped up toward the rider.

"Who the hell are you supposed to be?"

"Why you hide your face from us?" The Gray Hat referenced with a grin. "Show your damn face so we can know who you are, boy."

The rider stopped and started at the four men. His

face still hidden and his hands motionless on his sides. The man with the black hat stepped forward to the rider. Their faces near one another. The rider was not moved by the man's presence.

"Listen and listen good. Show us your face. You have nothing to lose. Besides your horse, of course."

"Enough of this." The White Hat yelled. "Quit playing hide and seek with us and show us your face. Who are you? Tell us your name."

"The Lone Outlaw." The Rider replied.

The four men shook in their boots. Taking minor steps back from the rider. They've heard of him across the Northern West. What he's done and the things he can do if necessary.

"It's… It's him." The Black Hat trembled in his speech. Pointing at the rider.

The rider swiftly moved his right hand, shoving his duster back and revealing his holster. From there, he fired shots at the man in the black hat, killing him with shots to the chest. He continued from there, turning toward the men in the brown and gray hats.

"Anything you wish to say?"

"You son of a-" The man in the brown hat yelled.

The rider fired once more, hitting the man in the brown hat through the chest. His eyes glared onto the man in the gray hat. Both standing completely still, their pistols directed to one another. The man in the gray hat quickened in his steps. Shuffling the pistol in his hand.

The rider watched him tremble.

"You're going to turn yourself over-"

The rider shot the man in the gray hat with the pistol and he fell to the ground, lying next to the men in the brown and black hats. Their hats sat on the ground motionless to the coming wind. The man in the white hat stared down at his fallen partners of their circle. His eyes moved slowly to face the rider, who's pistol was already aimed for him.

"You're the last man standing."

"What's it to you? You killed my boys!"

"Are you concerned?"

"Listen here, you're the guy we were discussing days prior. Yet, they were right. You brought yourself over to us and killed them. Killed the believers and left the unbeliever alive. All I ask of you right now is to turn yourself in for the crimes you've committed, and these murders are added to that list of crimes."

"I haven't done anything wrong."

"Have you now? Look around, boy! Look at what you've done to these three gentlemen."

"I've done this land a service. A great service."

"You've only committed three murders. That's all you've done right now. My boys were right, you're one crazy bastard."

"Good." The rider said.

"I have no choice." The White Hat said, reaching over to his holster. "You've given me no other choice, boy, but to put you down."

The rider fired at the man in the white hat. The gunshot blasted through his head, leaving a hole through the white hat as it fell to the ground. The dirt began to hover in the air as the wind started to pick up. The rider gazed around, feeling the chilling air coming. He looked down at the man in the white hat's body and spat on him.

"Justice and vengeance are all that is left for me in this world. I can only choose one of them. And I have chosen vengeance."

The rider climbed atop his horse and rode away as thunder started to roar in the clouds above the small town. The bodies of the four men remained on the ground as the rain started to fall.

RUNNING BEFORE TIME

Doctor Amadeus Omega worked himself to the bone inside his laboratory. The walls rattled as Amadeus worked. He worked and moved with haste. Amadeus wore his traditional white lab coat and goggles, somewhat smelly from nonstop labor. The laboratory was messy and yet clean. Clean to Amadeus' standards of clean. Much equipment laid on the floors and the desks. The messiness of the lab inspired Amadeus to create more, to study more, and to build more. Amadeus was finishing up a building process of a machine. The machine was large and wide. Built with steel and glass melted from interstellar sand. Amadeus turned toward a monitor placed against the wall. The monitor played the countdown for the machine to work. As the monitor counted down, the laboratory doors are slammed by a force unknown to Amadeus. But, he knew for sure who was behind the ramming. Amadeus looked toward the doors and back to the monitor.

"Should've sped up the countdown process." Amadeus said to himself. "Would've had this done if I had done so."

The doors shook as Amadeus jumped into his machine. Sitting down and buckling himself in the seat. The doors burst open and a group of soldiers barged in. Wearing black and red armor. Their faces covered by their helmet masks. The soldiers set themselves to surround Amadeus.

"Amadeus Omega! By the orders of Baron Eon, you are hereby placed under arrest!" The leading soldier demanded.

"I'm out of here." Amadeus said toward the soldiers. "Hey! Tell Eon I said to find me if he can!"

The door on Amadeus' machine closes itself. The machine emitted a bright flash of white light, blinding the soldiers from seeing Amadeus. The soldiers cover their eyes to avoid great damage from the light. The machine's roaring engine stung the soldiers' ears. Within mere seconds of the bright light and stinging sound, the light vanished, and Amadeus was gone. The soldiers regained their senses, scouting around the empty lab, Amadeus and his machine are nowhere in sight.

Amadeus sat inside the machine, moving through a wormhole in the time space continuum. He scouted the machine around the time loops, seeing alternate and parallel dimensions in time. The dimensions appeared to him like small videos playing without sound. The muteness of the images didn't disturb Amadeus, it only made him more curious to what could be happening in those realms. Amadeus inched closer toward one dimension in the time stream and smiled.

"There it is." Amadeus stared.

He turned the machine toward his left, entering the coming time loop. Traveling fast through the wormhole, Amadeus found himself in an open field. The machine makes itself a landing and stops atop the grassy plains. Amadeus exited the machine and gazed around the location. Seeing nothing but grass and plains. He nodded.

"Not the precise location I expected."

Amadeus dug into his coat pocket and pulled out a device. He pressed several buttons on the device and it responded with a message pertaining to the month and year Amadeus has traveled into. Amadeus read the device's response.

"Right on time." He said smiling. "Now, where could they be around this place?"

SCOUTING SESSION

Gage Hark walked through the corridor of Base 33. The secure underground prison which contains criminals and those of a greater grasp of power. Hark walked with a doctor who carried a clipboard, monitoring the criminals. The expressions of those behind the bars gave Hark deranged looks and he knew why. Yet, he could understand with his own scruffy expression. One like the experience of the field.

"What am I supposed to be looking at?" The Doctor asked.

"I'm looking for those who can accomplish the mission my boss has demanded."

"May I ask what this mission may imply to these criminals?"

"None of your concern, doctor."

The doctor nodded, and continued walking Hark down the corridor looking at the criminals left and right.

Hark is a man who's in service to the United States Military. One of their most prized lieutenants who's always accomplished his missions head-on. Hark took glances at the clipboard, catching the names of the criminals around him. Such names on the list– Thunderstorm, Rapidshine, G-Zero, The Hitman, Shadow Tiger, and Mistress Destroyer. Hark gleaned and pointed at one of the names on the list.

"Whose name is Doctor Streak?" Hark asked with concern. "Where did that come about?"

The doctor pointed to his right and Hark looked toward the cell. Inside sat a man dressed in a blue coat with a gold and black mask over his face. On the walls of his cell were drawings of bullets and firearms. Hark sensed he was a dedicated man in his craft. One who may have some possible use.

"Doctor Streak is a man who can target several shots with one blow."

"Eh, we already have someone in mind who's capable of those attributes." Hark mentioned. "But, I'll keep him on my list just in case."

They reached the end of the hallway and the doors closed. Hark followed the doctor to his office where they discussed the details concerning the criminals in the cells. Hark contacted his boss and told her of the criminals. After hanging up, Hark told the doctor his boss had declined all the following who sat in the corridor.

"Really?" The doctor said. "You require the use of any of them?"

"My boss said she's found some outside of this place who are far better than those in the cells."

"This world is growing rapidly I'll say."

"How so?"

"Those figures roaming around nowadays. You've seen them, haven't you?"

"You're talking about those heroes. Yeah. I've seen some evidence of their existence. Doesn't mean things will alter in our field."

"Oh, I believe things will alter. Perhaps even cease to exist. These heroes can accomplish things we mere mortals only dream of."

"And you believe all of that?"

"Yes. It's already happening globally. Soon, these figures will take our place in the fields of duty and we'll end up on the sidelines with everyone else. It is inevitable I'm afraid."

"I don't believe that." Hark said with dignity. "Not a damn bit of it."

"Then, please enlighten me, Lieutenant. I'm curious to know.'

"We can achieve what we desire. That is what I was taught in the military and that is what my boss demands. No need for petty dreams and soft speeches. Only the rough and rigid will survive this new world."

The doctor nodded. He stood up and approached

Hark slowly. He started Hark in the eyes, searching his mind and soul. Hark recognized the doctor's motive and only showed a small grin on his face.

"You can sit back down at your desk. I know who and what I am."

"Of that, I am aware." The doctor said returning to his desk. "What else do you require of me?"

"Nothing else. I'm returning to my boss's headquarters. Sort out this team dream there."

"Very well. Off you go, Lieutenant Hark."

Hark left Base 33, making his return to the boss' headquarters in the deep parts of the northern wilderness.

Hark entered the facility covered with guards dressed like Black Ops soldiers. Some wore alternative uniforms separating them from those outside. Hark walked inside past others such as himself, all of whom were dressed in suits and ties. They glanced at Hark and his military uniform and scoffed. Hark chucked under his breath at the suits. He continued moving in his military strut and came upon his boss' office. He entered, and he saw his boss at the desk.

"I've arrived, boss."

His boss is known across the underground circle as A.B., but her full name is Adrian Brown. Adrian stood up from the desk and circled Hark in the office. She nodded and required of him to sit and he sat. She returned to her desk and sat, facing Hark. Hark nodded stiffly and swallowed.

"You turned down those who were offered."

"I did it for good reason, Hark. A reason that will benefit all of us in this facility and will benefit the world as we see it."

"You've found some out there? Some of those who may be of use?"

"Of great use." Adrian said with determination in her voice. "I've located nine of them across the world and their attributes will fare well in our advantage."

"They're not those heroic figures roaming around, are they?"

"Of course not. We needed those of the criminal element and the paid price would bring in the rest."

"You're talking of mercenaries." Hark jumped. "You have mercenaries in your sights?"

"They're highly valuable to the cause and they will help us greatly." Adrian smiled.

"I could bring in some of my partners in the force and we could handle this mission you have set up. We can get it done by nightfall and no one will see us coming and going. Why do you require the use of criminals and mercenaries anyway? Why does the mission need them?"

"You want to know why, Hark?"

"Obviously. If possible."

"The criminals and the mercenaries do not have the sensitivity and the care you and your force buddies have. They will do the mission as planned and they will complete it. Therefore, they will learn how this world has changed and how it works under our rule."

Hark nodded. He understood his boss' motives to the mission and even though he doesn't agree with her methods, he has great respect for Adrian and what she has done throughout her career. He took a moment to breathe while Adrian looked through a folder. She closed the folder, sliding it over to Hark. He eyed the folder and reached to grab it. Adrian agreed for him to open the folder. Hark opened it and looked at the details inside. He was somewhat astonished and yet trembled.

"You cannot be serious about this." Hark wondered.

"I am serious. As serious as an ant in the summer. They will be the team. Whether they agree or not."

Hark closed the folder and laid it on the desk. Adrian pointed toward it with a glare in her eyes.

"You'll need to take that with you on your journey."

"My journey?"

"I'm sending you to go out there and recruit them. All of them?"

"Wait. Hold on. Some of them are difficult to track. How am I supposed to run into them? Especially in the same distance as those heroes?"

"You'll find a way. As you've always done. Treat it as a military expedition. You're familiar with them I assume."

Hark agreed and grabbed the folder. He stood up and nodded toward Adrian, leaving the office he walked outside and grabbed a hold of one of their jeeps. He took another peek at the folder and sighed.

"This will be crazy."

IN TIME, THEY WILL KNOW

"The world has changed and is changing continually. That is what I've been told and what I have seen."

Walking out of the shadows is a man, clocked in all white with a black helmet covering his entire head and face. Walking out, he raised his hands over his head, pulling the hood of the cloak over the helmet. The eyes of the helmet glow a bright white and the man vanished.

"From the ages of the mythical Swordman of Retropolis to the titagod, Powerman of Enigma City, The Nano Man of Newark, the resurrected soldier from Toronto, the Millennium God from a distant realm, A man who can transform into a monster with great power and might. Even then, there are others such as the doctor who proclaims himself the Supreme Enchanter, the young astonishing hero in Los Angeles, an Atlantean king who is prepared to war with his own kind, a clever scientist who has learn to shrink himself to an atom's size."

The man warped through a wormhole, traveling through dimensions within the universe itself. The traveling didn't harm him as the helmet gave him the guidance he needed to reach his destination.

"Meanwhile, there are those of the other side. Such like the Chaser of Souls, the Astral entity of the darkness. The brash casino owner part-time hero of Las Vegas, the protector of the Avago Land, another one of Chicago's guardians who deems himself a devil, a pair of two men with no similar abilities who use their strength to achieve profit. Such I have seen, and such will I see again,"

He reached a spot in the wormhole and extended his hand toward it. He pulled the wall of the wormhole apart and went through the makeshift exit. Through the exit, the man found himself in the midst of a rural town. He knew the town very well and confirmed it with a nod.

"I have not forgotten about the ones of many kinds. The young sly detective named after a fairy tale figure, one young man who's recruited into a secret agency unaware of his duties, the famed Spirit-Seeker who's learning of this expanded realm, the spiritual assassin of Chicago. The returning king of Mekeopia, an enraged man dealing with the loss of his humanity. They are those such like the others. A cometh of the near future."

The man warped through the rural town, searching. Looking for something or someone. He searched every home and every structure capable of holding humans. The helmet glowed a bright white he made his search.

"In that future, there will be those such like the Unholy Knight trying to redeem his spirit from the evil, the con man who uses magic for fame and fortune only to have it return to him sevenfold in the future, a pair of nubreeds who will learn to cope with their circumstances and avoid the hatred of those outside their perimeter, a royal family whose heritage reaches the farthest stars in the second heaven. A lone outlaw of the past whose actions will determine many futures. A time-traveling doctor who's making his way to this present timeline to recruit those who will need the assistance, and a group of criminals who look to get their way with anyone as possible as it may be."

The man stopped at one location. A church. The man entered the church and inside sat a man as the front pew. He was panting for air and wiping the sweat from his face. The man levitated toward him. The man at the pew turned back, seeing the cloaked figure. He jolted out of his seat and fell to the floor.

"Do not fear me, mortal."

"Please, don't kill me!" The man screamed.

"I will not kill you." The cloaked figure declared.

"Then, what do you want with me?"

"I want you to remember."

"Remember what?"

"Remember this face and all those I have spoken this

night. Once you understand, the way will show itself before you."

"I don't understand." The man questioned. "What way?"

"In time, they will know." The cloaked figure said, turning away.

"Who are they?"

"You already know."

The cloaked figure vanished through a flashing light which formed the symbol of Helven. Leaving the man on the floor gazing around. Rubbing his eyes, he stood up and looked around again. He had no sight of the cloaked figure in his presence. He immediate ran out of the church to tell others of his encounter with the Specter Errant.

BE ON THE LOOKOUT FOR
THE UPCOMING SERIALS.

HALLOW
SWORD™

CHOSEN SON

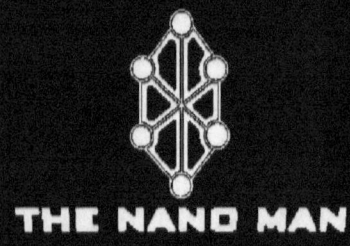

THE NANO MAN

COMMANDER
NORLAND

THE
UNSTOPPABLE
BEAST

AND MANY OTHERS BEGINNING IN APRIL.
EXCLUSIVELY ON DARKTITANENTERTAINMENT.COM

www.ingramcontent.com/pod-product-compliance
Lightning Source LLC
Chambersburg PA
CBHW021010120726
47905CB00009B/2941